THE MYSTERIOUS WU FANG:
THE CASE OF THE BLACK LOTUS

THE CASE OF
THE BLACK LOTUS

By Robert J. Hogan

ALTUS PRESS • 2017

EDITED AND DESIGNED BY

Matthew Moring

PUBLISHING HISTORY

"The Case of the Black Lotus" originally appeared in the February, 1936 (Vol. 2, No. 2) issue of *The Mysterious Wu Fang* magazine. Copyright 1936 by Popular Publications, Inc. Copyright renewed 1963 and assigned to Steeger Properties, LLC. All rights reserved.

CHAPTER 1
THE NOTE ON THE
CHOPSTICKS

J ERRY HAZARD was sitting at his desk in the office of the McNulty News Syndicate. His fingers were flying over the typewriter keys as he finished the last of a series of articles on the explorations of his friend, Rod Carson, the famous young archaeologist. His square-jawed face was haggard from worry, and his thoughts as he wrote the last paragraph were not on the contents of his article, but on Mohra, the dark, exotically beautiful girl who was at this moment in the power of his arch enemy, Wu Fang.

As he reached the end of the last sentence, he punched the period key with savage finality and snuffed out the cigarette he had been smoking. He leaned back in his chair, took a long breath, and stretched.

Now that the day's work was finished, he would do the same thing he had been doing every night for more than two weeks; go down to Chinatown and continue his search for Mohra. Never would he rest until he had found her and taken her away with him, forever—out of the clutches of Wu Fang.

As he strode from the chief's office, a friendly voice called to him.

"Jerry, come here."

It was another reporter, seeking his attention.

Absently, Hazard walked to the other desk, where a new magazine was pushed in front of him.

"It's an advance copy of the Weekly Post," the reporter said.

Hazard felft the fingers bite
deep into his flesh.

"I received it only a half hour ago. It doesn't hit the stands until Tuesday."

At first glance, Hazard noticed the magazine was open to an article entitled "Secret Orders of the Orient. By Ming Lee."

"I know you're interested in Chink stuff," the reporter said. "Thought maybe you'd like to see this."

Hazard picked up the magazine and scanned the first paragraph.

"Yeh," he said, "thanks."

With that, he tucked the magazine under his arm and started again for his hat and coat.

"Hey," the reporter called, "I didn't say I'd give it to you. I'm only lending it."

Hazard turned without a word, his eyes still riveted on the first few lines of the article. He picked a handful of change from his pocket, lifted his eyes from the magazine long enough to sort out the proper coin and toss it on the table.

"I might forget to bring it back," he explained.

He attempted to read the article outside in the drizzling rain as he waited on the curb for a cab; but the light cast by the street lamps was too dim. When a cab finally arrived, he climbed in and gave the driver his order.

"Mott Street," he said.

"Any particular number?" the driver asked as he flicked the meter.

"No, just so it's Chinatown."

Switching on the dome light, Hazard began perusing the article. Pictures of Chinese parades stood out on the page, along with one of the author, Ming Lee, attired in native costume, an ordinary little Chinaman, hollow cheeked and slant eyed.

Various paragraphs stood out before him as he raced through the article, particularly those concerning the Chang Li and its secrets.

"The Chang Li," the article read, "was formed more than two thousand years ago as a secret order of mandarins. It was established originally for political purposes by certain people who wished to hold the influence in China.

"It has many interesting ceremonies, one of which is the march of the *kwan*. The main ceremony of this festival is the parade through the streets, in which the members bear aloft a Chinese casket containing the effigy of Sun Hu Chek, who was emperor of China more than one thousand years ago. It was he who nearly caused the downfall of the Chang Li during his reign. But the Chang Li influence was victorious in the end and Sun Hu Chek was overthrown. Now the great festival of the Chang Li is dedicated to the memory of its victory over the emperor.

"Directly following the Chinese casket as it is born through the streets is a long dragon covering the head and shoulders of two dozen marchers.

"The Chang Li is one of the most secret orders in the world. Many Chinese participate, but their identity remains unknown to the average oriental. In this parade, the members disguise themselves by wearing large heads resembling various gods.

"At the end of the ceremony, the casket is taken to the temple of Chang Li, a secret place that is open only to members of the order. Here, on the altar before an image of the great god, the casket and the effigy of Sun Hu Chek within, is burned with great ceremony as a sacrifice.

"One of the most jealously guarded secrets of the Chang Li is the propagation and growth of its secret flower, the black lotus. Members of the Chang Li are the only ones in the world who know this secret of horticultural cross-breeding. So it is safe to say that when one finds black lotus growing in the garden of a Chinaman, he is a member of this great secret order of the Chang Li."

Hazard's cab drew up in the middle of Mott Street in the heart of New York's Chinatown. The newspaper man, not being particularly impressed, dropped the magazine on the seat, stepped out of the cab, and paid the driver.

As he stood for a few minutes on the curb, Chinese in both Oriental and Occidental garb walked up and down the street, taking no notice of him.

Many nights he had stood there and watched this throng when he first arrived in Chinatown, hoping vainly that he might catch a glimpse of Mohra.

A half hour passed. Hazard tossed his sixth cigarette in the gutter and walked down Mott Street until he came to Pell, the narrow thoroughfare where all the Chinese ceremonies were held.

A few doors from the corner, he paused before a dark entrance—where a flight of steep stairs dropped into the basement of the building. Just over the stairs on a level with the sidewalk was a little sign. Hazard did not know the meaning of the individual characters, but he knew that it advertised the place of Ling Toi. He had been there on several evenings before.

HE PUSHED open the door and stepped into a little underground restaurant. Of the four tables in the place, only one was occupied at the moment. Two Chinese in native garb sat opposite each other, talking in Cantonese.

As Hazard entered, the conversation ceased, abruptly. An air of tense suspicion seemed suddenly to fill the place.

A little Chinaman with a round, beaming face came shuffling toward him from the kitchen at the back. Hazard saw his eyes flash toward the two other Chinamen at the table; but only for an instant, the genial smile never leaving the plump proprietor's face.

"Good evening," he greeted the newspaper man. "Velly glad see you. You clum take this table?"

Hazard nodded and grinned.

"Good evening, Ling Toi," he said. "What's good on the menu?"

The proprietor rubbed his hands and his beaming moon-like face grinned more expansively than ever.

"Glot velry good chop suey tonight with Chinese fish," he said. "Velly good."

Hazard hesitated.

"Chinese fish,' he repeated thoughtfully. "Think I'd like it?"

The head of the Chinaman bobbed eagerly.

"You like very much," he said emphatically. "You try him?"

"All right," Hazard nodded. "Bring it on."

"And tea? Tea with lemon?"

"That's right," Hazard said. "You've got a good memory, Ling Toi."

"Thank you. You not have to wait velly long."

Ling Toi, still beaming broadly, shuffled back to the kitchen.

A lapse of perhaps ten minutes occurred and then Ling Toi reentered, bearing a huge bowl of steaming chop suey in his left hand and a cup of tea in his right. He set the food down before Hazard and the newspaper man glanced at it.

He had been wondering as he sat there how he would eat this food with chop sticks like the Chinese at the other table were using, apparently with great dexterity. He looked at the chop sticks, frowned, and glanced up at Ling Toi.

"I thought," he began.

But that was as far as he got. Something in the expression of the Chinese proprietor warned him to stop. Ling Toi gave him a sly wink and with a slight shake of his head, he said, "You like velly much. Chop suey velly good with sticks."

"Yes," Hazard nodded, a little bewildered. "Sure, of course."

"You try him that way. I wait and see how you get along."

And now for the first time, Hazard noticed that Ling Toi was standing so that he was between Hazard and the two men at the front table. The newspaper men frowned again. Something was up.

Ling Toi was beaming once more as he nodded encouragement.

"You try him," he repeated.

"O.K.?" Hazard said. "Here goes."

With that, he drew out the chop sticks from where they were

stuck in the bowl of chop suey. Then, as he placed them between his fingers in the customary Chinese fashion, he saw something small and white in the end of one of the sticks. A slip of folded paper, slightly soaked with the juice of the food.

Carrying along the bantering conversation that Ling Toi had begun, Hazard quickly plucked out the paper with his left hand, dipped the chop sticks into the bowl and brought them to his lips with a very scant portion of the chop suey between them.

"M'm, this is good this way," he said.

"Yes, velly good with sticks," Ling Toi agreed.

He proceeded to wipe off the other side of the table with his apron, stalling for time so that he could remain between Hazard and the other two Chinamen, while the newspaper man unfolded the paper and scanned the few words that were scrawled on it in English:

WAIT UNTIL TWO MEN GONE.

He dropped the paper into his pocket, nodded to Ling Toi that he understood, and dipped the chop sticks into the bowl again. This time, he managed to get hold of a larger portion.

"Yes," he said, "this is fine. I'm glad you made me use these chop sticks, Ling Toi."

"I velly glad you like," Ling Toi replied.

Then the chubby Chinese proprietor turned and went back into the kitchen.

Out of the corner of his eye, Hazard saw the two yellow men glancing at him now and then as he ate, but he pretended not to notice.

When they had finished their meal, Ling Toi came in and spoke a few words to them in Chinese in the usual manner of the genial host. Then they paid their bill and went out.

Ling Toi watched them climb the steps outside the door. Then he turned to Hazard and jerked his head toward the steps.

"You know them?" he asked.

Hazard shook his head.

"Never saw them before in my life that I can remember," he said.

"Them velly bad men," Ling Toi said. "I hear them say somebody die tonight."

"That's not out of the ordinary for Chinatown, is it?" Hazard asked. "If I were a reporter covering this beat, I suppose I ought to follow them so I could actually see the murder committed."

But his light-heartedness faded at Toi's next words.

"They say somebody die tonight as a sacrifice. A girl."

Jerry Hazard snapped bolt upright in his chair.

"What's that?" he demanded.

The head of the little proprietor bobbed up and down.

"**THEY NOT** know I hear them," he said. "They talk about very beautiful girl going to be sacrificed. White girl. The fat one, I hear him say if he could rescue her from sacrifice, he would keep her for himself."

"Good Lord," breathed Hazard, half aloud. "You—you—" He was almost afraid to ask that question. "You didn't hear them mention her name, did you."

"No, Mr. Hazard," Ling Toi, said, shaking his head. "Not hear name of girl."

Suddenly what appetite Hazard had when he entered the place was gone.

"Look here," he said, leaning forward excitedly. "Did you hear them mention any other name?"

"Hear one name," Ling Toi told him.

"What was it?"

"They mentioned tea importer. His name Ah Joy."

"I know where his place is," Hazard said, half rising. "Do you know anything about him?"

Ling Toi shook his head.

"No," he said, "but I hear talk that Ah Joy not make all his money importing tea."

"That wouldn't surprise me in the least," Hazard said. "Here—" He plunged his hand into his pocket, brought out a dollar bill, and stuffed it into the fat palm of Ling Toi. "Keep the change," he said, "and thanks a lot. I'll be shoving along."

"You go to see Ah Joy?"

Hazard gave a decisive nod.

"You're right. I'm going to see him," he said. "And if that bird knows anything about Mohra and won't tell me, so help me, I'll—"

"Do not do anything too quickly," Ling Toi warned. "There is a proverb of your own that has to do with this—"

Hazard was already half way to the door, but Ling Toi caught him by the arm.

"There is something about the place of Ah Joy that you should know," he said. "He closes his shop at six. It is long past that hour now. But there is a narrow alley beside the building where he has his shop. I believe any secret passage is made in and out of that building from the alley to the little yard behind. You would do well to go there and watch, keeping deep in shadows."

Then Ling Toi let him go.

"Thanks a lot," Hazard said again. "Maybe I'll take that advice."

He went out into the drizzling night, walked back to Mott Street and turned left. In the dim light that burned along the street, he could just barely make out the sign, "Ah Joy, Importer of Tea." In the windows of the shop were piled little straw-covered bales of tea for exhibition. Peering through the windows in the front revealed nothing, but the pitch blackness within.

A feeling of helplessness rushed over him, for he hadn't the slightest doubt that Mohra was confined within that building. He was absolutely certain that the beautiful white girl referred to by the Chinaman as that night's sacrifice was his Mohra.

In spite of all obstacles he would get underground into the passages that honeycombed the bottom of Chinatown. If Mohra was where she could be reached at all, he could find her.

Half a block farther on, he crossed the street to Ah Joy's shop, and turned the knob. Yes, the door was locked all right.

A surge of baffled rage flooded over him for an instant. He doubled his fist to knock furiously on the door and demand to see Ah Joy. He would face him and—

Then his mind flashed abruptly to the words of caution that Ling Toi had spoken. Ah Joy was apparently a dangerous person if stories concerning him were true.

With that thought in mind, Hazard stepped away from the

door to the sidewalk and approached the narrow passageway at the side of the building. As he peered into that pitch-dark alley, he could hear the thud, thud, thud of water dripping from the roof three stories above.

The newspaper man stepped into the alley, which was barely wide enough to walk through without turning sidewise.

In the darkness, he thought he could see a window or two overhead on either side, but he couldn't be sure. He felt along the walls with his hands as he made his way on tip toe, moving cautiously as Ling Toi had suggested.

Half way down the alley, he felt a doorway. He tried the door but it was locked. Bracing himself between the walls with his shoulder against the heavy door, he put his weight against it. But the door wouldn't yield a fraction of an inch.

He went on. The alley ran a little more than a hundred feet until it reached a brick wall, perhaps six feet high which enclosed a small court.

At the rear of the building, Hazard found another door. His heart leaped as he turned the knob, and the door opened easily.

He slipped inside and tensed in the darkness. Where was he heading? Mohra should be there, somewhere. Of that, he was sure.

The atmosphere was tinged with smells of the orient, musty, dank and mingled with incense.

FOR A long moment he stood there listening, gun clutched tightly in his hand, finger against the trigger, ready to shoot at an instant's notice. The deathly stillness was appalling.

A door to the right swung open easily before him, almost too easily, as though the way had been left open to him.

If this were a trap to draw him into the lair of Wu Fang or some other underworld yellow men, they'd have to work fast to stop him. Dead Chinamen would certainly line his path.

He felt about over the threshold for a footing. Gingerly, he let himself down slowly, feeling, feeling. His foot settled solidly on a step.

Fourteen steps to the bottom he counted. The smell of earth, wet stone and mold mingled with the unmistakable odor of incense. Hazard's hands groped along the walls as he descended deeper and deeper into the earth with every step.

Up to now he had not lighted his flashlight, lest it disclose his purpose. But now he had come, apparently, to the end of the passage, and there was nothing more except this hole.

Leaning over, he snapped on the flash, the beam revealing the dank, dark pit.

Hazard saw things clearly now that he was at the brink of a small underground room, the floor of which was perhaps fifteen feet below the level of the passage.

Hazard gasped as he stared down at what was clearly a trap. This passage had been left open to foil any intruder. Had Hazard not felt his way through the dark corridor, he would have plunged to his death.

But he must get down. Leaning farther over the edge, he tried to find the downward wall with his light. The beam traveled inward almost under him and now he saw that there were iron bars built in the stone wall, with iron rings at the side of the drop. It was by this means, then, that those entering through the door lowered themselves into the secret chamber.

Instantly Hazard proceeded to lower himself. He tested the iron ring, and the bars as he went down. They were all solid and free of rust, which meant they were used regularly.

Reaching the bottom, he swung his light about the small, well-like enclosure, disclosing an opening at the far end.

But a sound came that froze him in his tracks.

Creak! Creak!

Someone was coming behind him.

Jerry Hazard was running now, down the corridor ahead of him. He must find where this led to; find a place to hide before that other figure caught up with him.

Something brushed his arm as he raced on. Hazard's entire body broke out in a cold sweat. He suddenly realized that his flashlight was gone. Had he dropped it? Or had it been knocked from his hand? Had someone—some underworld thing of mystery with cat eyes, snatched it from him as he raced by?

He spun round and his automatic whirled with him, pointing at the place where he thought the flashlight had vanished.

Stark fear for Mohra and sudden panic blanked his reason, forced him to pull the trigger of his gun.

Blam!

But the only answering sound was the *ping* of his bullet as it ricocheted off the stone wall.

Hazard was running again, running blindly. From the other end of the corridor there came a faint cry, more of astonishment than pain.

Next he heard the thud of running feet behind him.

Blam!

The gun in his right hand suddenly vanished, as though a magnet had snatched it from his grasp. He felt a figure against him for an instant—in a rapid passing at his back.

Desperately, he raced toward that light ahead of him. From behind it came the sound of a voice.

Bong!

A gong sounded, deep, mellow and weird, echoing and vibrating throughout the passage.

A muffled cry of fear and torment sounded as Hazard whirled around the corner of an archway and into a small enclosure, decorated ornately in the fashion of the orient.

But what held him spell bound—stopped him aghast in his tracks—were the half dozen grotesque figures in the room. Great contorted faces were leering at him, and as he leaped into the center of the throng, he felt the certainty that behind one of those ghastly faces, Wu Fang, the Dragon Lord of Crime, was hiding.

A silken drape was suddenly hurled through the air by a skillful hand and landed in a crumpled heap on the floor.

But Hazard was leaping over that at a figure, thin and gaunt, tall and with narrow shoulders—like Wu Fang. His fists were clenched and ready to fly, but they never landed.

Powerful hands seized him from behind, suddenly, with the quality of steel.

Struggling like a mad man, Hazard hurled his threats at the yellow men.

"I've come to get Mohra," he cried, "and I'm going to get her if I have to—"

His voice broke as something pricked him in the back and a numb feeling spread over him. And as he slowly faded into unconsciousness, he heard a voice.

"We know nothing of Mohra. She is not here, and this is none of your affair."

THEN EVERYTHING faded into blackness, stealing Hazard's senses until he awoke with rain drizzling down on him.

Opening his eyes, he sat up. Everything was jumbled. However, he was sure of two things. In his left hand was his flashlight, in his other rested his automatic.

Unsteadily, he struggled to his feet. Now he realized he was in a back alley. And with sudden recollection, recognized it as the very alley from which he had entered the back door of Ah Joy's building.

He fumbled with the automatic, only to find the clip and cartridge missing.

Reaching the back door he slammed it open, and started down the steps as he had before. But something had changed all that. There was a blank, solid wall in front of him, a mysterious wall that had closed in since his earlier entrance.

Still baffled and dizzy, he turned out into the back of the alley once more. He couldn't understand all this. Why had they placed him in the alley with his gun and the flashlight? They certainly hadn't meant to kill him. They had rendered him unconscious because he had been sticking his nose in some place where he wasn't wanted. He was suddenly satisfied that Mohra was not in there. There had been something about that firm Chinese voice that convinced him.

But what of that figure huddled beneath the silk drape that had been so quickly thrown over it? Perhaps that was—

Hazard shook his head and turned, half insane with panic, toward the street end of the alley.

He tensed as he heard a sound, the faintest indication of a bolt sliding to and fro. Jerry Hazard made a sudden resolve. This was the first time that he had anything definite to tell Val Kildare, the government agent with whom he worked against Wu Fang. Now he had two things to tell. A beautiful white girl was to be sacrificed in Chinatown tonight and the name of Ah Joy had been mentioned in connection with it.

He started down the alley, but as he reached the place where the two doors, one from either side of the buildings, opened almost opposite each other, his foot struck something hard and round. It felt like the leg of a human being.

His hands dove into his pockets and came out, a flash light in the left, an automatic in the right. The beam from his flash light shone down on the thing on the ground. A face with dull, staring eyes was turned up at him, its expression horribly contorted. Strange, that face seemed familiar. He tried to think where he had seen it before. Then he had it. It was Ming Lee, author of that article in the Weekly Post, concerning the Chang Li.

This, then had been the figure huddled on the floor under the silk draping.

CHAPTER 2
BLACK LOTUS DEATH

THE SPACE in the alley was so cramped that Jerry Hazard had to straddle the corpse in order to examine it more closely.

Ming Lee's body was stretched out straight and his hands were folded over his chest. Hazard saw that one of those hands clutched something, a flower, large, black, and beautiful.

The newspaper man's mind flashed back to the article this man had written. He had said that the sacred flower of the order of Chang Li was the black lotus. And this was a black lotus that he clutched in his lifeless hand.

The flower exuded a strange odor, not unlike a fragrant water lily. He bent down a little farther so that his nostrils would be nearer the origin of the fragrance. Then caution prompted him to recoil. This sacred black lotus might have had something to do with the death of Ming Lee. Could it be possible that there was death in that beautiful black blossom?

He rose to his feet, horror gripping his very soul. He hesitated for a moment. Val Kildare should know about this. He would go and tell him at once.

The subway train that he took uptown seemed to move with incredible laziness. He sat tense on the edge of his seat and the moment it stopped at his station, he dashed out and up the stairs.

He found Kildare as he had expected at the Explorer's Club. An old friend of both Hazard and Kildare was there with him.

Rod Carson, famous young archaeologist and explorer, was standing in front of Kildare who was just in the act of rising from his chair. It was Carson who spoke first.

"You're just in time, Jerry," he said. "I was afraid I wouldn't be able to say goodbye to you. I'm pulling out for parts unknown as usual."

"Listen," Hazard cried, "you won't want to go now, Rod, when I tell you what's come up."

Rod Carson was about Hazard's height and build. His face was a little squarer than the newspaper man's and his jaw a bit more rock-like. He frowned suddenly but before he could speak, Val Kildare, the lean, broad-shouldered former government man smiled at Hazard and spoke.

"Apparently, Jerry, you've been hanging about Chinatown," he said. "What's up now?"

"Plenty," Hazard said, still breathing a little rapidly from his recent exertion. "Tonight something is going to happen. In fact, something has already happened. I mean—"

Hazard suddenly felt his whole body grow tense.

"You mean Mohra?" Kildare asked quickly. "You've found traces of her?"

Hazard hesitated for a moment. Something rose in his throat and choked him.

Rod Carson laid a gentle hand on his shoulder and advised in his characteristic clipped speech, "Take it easy old man. What is it?"

"I think so," Hazard said. "I'm sure of it. She—" he paused

a moment to fight down that lump in his throat again— "she's going to be sacrificed tonight."

"Sacrificed?" Kildare and Carson blurted in the same breath.

"That's impossible," Carson flared. "This is a civilized country. We—"

"Dammit, I tell you it's not impossible," Kildare cut in. For a moment the usual calm of the government man gave way to tense excitement. Then with apparent effort, he relaxed and motioned Hazard to a chair.

"Come on, Jerry," he said. "Sit down and let's talk this thing over." He turned to Carson and asked, "You're not in such a great hurry to be off, are you, Rod?"

Carson shook his head.

"No," he said, "I'm sitting in on this. My trip can wait."

"Good," Kildare nodded. "Now," he suggested, turning his

calm, gray eyes on Hazard, "start at the beginning and tell us what you know."

"Something happened when I left the office tonight and started for Chinatown," Hazard began. "One of the boys gave me an advance copy of the Weekly Post. It had an article by a Chinaman named Ming Lee. I read it in the cab on the way to Chinatown. It concerns the secrets of various organizations, particularly the Chang Li of which I believe Ming Lee was a member."

"Yes," Kildare nodded, "I read that article."

Hazard's eyes flashed open in surprise.

"You read it?" he said.

"Yes," Kildare told him, "I read it a little over a month ago before it went to press."

"But I don't see—" Hazard began.

"The editors of the Weekly Post asked me to read it and pass judgment on it," Kildare explained. "They knew I was interested in the Chinese angle and they wanted my opinion as to whether they would run into trouble if they printed it. It was very interesting, I thought."

"And you told them to go ahead and print it?" Carson asked.

"Yes, of course," Kildare said. "Why not? I did warn them, however, to tell Ming Lee that he had better go in hiding for the rest of his life after the article came out in print."

Hazard opened his mouth to speak, but Kildare leaned back and held up a restraining hand.

"Don't tell me yet that Ming Lee is dead," he said. "Tell me what led up to your finding him."

Hazard stared at the government man in amazement.

"HOW IN the name of time do you know this?" he demanded. "It just happened less than an hour ago and you've been here all that time. Did you get a telephone call or something?"

"No," Kildare said. "It isn't very difficult to put two and two together and make four, you know. After all, I was afraid Ming Lee wouldn't take my advice—soon enough. Apparently, someone in Chinatown got hold of an advance copy of the Weekly Post, too. But go on and tell me how everything developed from the beginning. What did you learn about Mohra?"

Hazard told him what the proprietor of the little restaurant had said concerning the two Chinese in his shop. Next, he explained the incident in the alley beside Ah Joy's tea shop. "I knew it was Ming Lee the minute I got a light on his face. But here's the queer part of it. Ming Lee was lying on his back, his hands folded across his chest and in his hands was a black lotus."

"A black lotus!" Rod Carson exclaimed. "Look here, there isn't any such thing. Not that I ever heard of anyway, and I've been in every country in the world where they grow lotus flowers."

"Nevertheless," Kildare cut in, "there is such a thing as a black lotus. I remembered it was mentioned in the article in the Weekly Post and on one or two occasions I have seen the black lotus growing in the private gardens of the wealthy yellow men in Chinatown. The black lotus is the sacred flower of the Chang Li, isn't it, Jerry?"

"Right," Hazard nodded.

"And what did you do with the body?" Kildare asked. "Did you report his death to the police?"

"No," Hazard replied, shaking his head. "I thought of it, but I knew he was dead and was sure that no good would come

His flash revealed a dead
man on the ground.

from reporting it. Besides, I wanted you to see things just as they were."

"Good," Kildare said. "Let's go have a look at the body."

As the government man rose from trig chair, there was a commotion outside the club rooms. A page boy could be heard saying, "But I tell you, we don't allow paper selling in here."

"I didn't come here to sell papers," a familiar boyish voice protested. "I want to see Mr. Kildare or Jerry Hazard or Mr. Carson."

Jerry Hazard pricked up his ears.

"That voice sounded like Cappy," he said.

He was on his feet in an instant and the three of them strode out into the club lobby. Cappy stood at the entrance, tousle-headed, excited, and holding a bunch of papers under his arm. The moment he saw Hazard, he ducked under the page boy's arm and ran up to him.

"Jerry, Jerry," he exploded, "I found out something. The papers weren't going so good around my corner so I went down to Chinatown. I knew you were down there and I thought I might see you and sell some papers, too. When I got there, I met a Chinese boy I know. He's a Boy Scout, too. He told me he had just heard that they're going to hold a big parade in Pell Street at midnight."

"A parade!" Hazard cried.

"What kind of a parade, Cappy?" Kildare asked.

"Well, it's some land of a snaky thing from what Chink told me. Something about their wearing big heads to represent spirits and things. Then they've got a dragon that the marchers carry on their shoulders and there's a coffin at the head of the procession. They're going to make some kind of a sacrifice tonight."

A sudden hush fell over the three men. Cappy's eyes sparkled with excitement.

"Did I tell you something you wanted to know, Mr. Kildare?"

"Indeed you did. Cappy," Kildare nodded. "You say this is going to take pace at midnight in Pell Street?"

"Yes, sir, that's what Chink said," Cappy replied.

Kildare glanced at his watch.

"That's fine," he said. "There's plenty of time between now and then. We'll see what we can do."

The government man flipped Cappy a half dollar and the boy caught it expertly.

"But gee, Mr. Kildare," he argued, "I didn't expect to get paid for this. All I wanted to do was help."

"You've done more by telling us what you have, son," Kildare smiled, "than you can imagine. That half dollar isn't given as pay. That's—shall we call it expense money? You don't ride on subways for nothing, you know. Now all three of us have very important work to do and you've got a big bundle of papers to sell—so run along and if you want to get hold of me you can call the Mulberry Street police station."

"Yes, sir," Cappy said. He shot a glance at Hazard. "Gee, Jerry," he said, "I hope you find Mohra."

"We've got to," Hazard choked grimly.

Then Cappy stepped into an elevator and the door clanged behind him. Hazard felt his muscles twitch. His fingers were

26

shaking. A parade at midnight. A casket. Sacrifice. That meant only one thing to him.

"Jove," Kildare exploded, that was a lucky break to get the information at this time. Apparently, this is the parade of the Chinatown chapter of the Chang Li, marking the opening of the festival in honor of their victory over the emperor Sun Hu Chek more than a thousand years ago. That casket is supposed to contain the effigy of Sun Hu Chek."

Hazard clenched his teeth, laid one trembling hand on the automatic in his pocket. Before the night was over, somebody was going to get that if things didn't go his way.

"Jerry," Kildare snapped, "for your own good, you'd better let me have that gun. You'll get in trouble with it, keyed up as you are."

"I'll be O.K.," Hazard replied stubbornly, making a desperate effort to calm his jittery nerves.

BUT KILDARE continued to insist on taking the gun. He reached into Hazard's pocket, took out the automatic and dropped it into his own.

"If we get into a real tough spot, I'll give it to you, Jerry," he promised. "And now, we'd better get down to Chinatown. I have one stop to make before we reach there."

That one stop was at the Mulberry Street police station. Hazard heard Kildare tell the captain about the parade.

"I don't think it would be a bad idea if you had fifty or a hundred cops on Pell Street tonight," the government man suggested.

The captain nodded.

"Right you are," he said. "How did you know it was going to come off tonight?"

Kildare shrugged.

"It must be because I'm a seventh son of a seventh son," he smiled.

The captain grinned.

"That isn't exactly what I've heard some of the boys call you," he admitted, "but thanks for the tip anyway."

Kildare turned to go but then, apparently as an afterthought, he faced the captain again and said, "Oh, by the way, captain, I forgot to tell you that there has been a murder down on Mott Street. The body has been lying in an alley almost an hour now. Funny, I almost forgot about it."

"A murder!" the captain boomed. "And you say the body has been lying there over an hour and you haven't told us about it?"

Kildare feigned embarrassment as he answered, "Well, you see, after I heard about the murder, this affair of the parade came up and the other thing quite slipped my mind for the time being."

The captain eyed him skeptically.

"Say, what are you giving me?" he demanded. "You've got a special reason why you haven't told me about this murder before."

Kildare, Hazard, and Carson rode with the police to Mott Street. Hazard directed them to the alley beside Ah Joy's tea shop.

As Kildare bent down beside the body, there was a sudden exclamation from one of the officers.

"For the love of Mike, look at the way he's laid out. A lily in his hand and everything."

"Yeh," said the other cop, "and from the size of him, he doesn't look any bigger than a peanut. It's a wonder some stray dog hasn't dragged him home."

The first cop reached down for the black lotus flower but Kildare pushed him away.

"I wouldn't do that," he suggested. "We don't know yet what caused his death. This flower, the black lotus, is very rare and it's possible that—"

"You mean," the cop interrupted, "that maybe he got a sniff of this flower and that's what killed him?"

"There's no telling," Kildare said with a shrug.

"Say listen," the cop boomed, "you'll have us reading fairy stories before we get through with this."

"Well," Kildare ventured, "maybe you'd rather not be able to read at all."

Both cops were bending over watching Kildare as he bared the Chinaman's chest.

"Can't find a thing," he said. "There isn't a mark on him."

"Maybe," suggested one of the cops, "they wanted you to think that this guy died of heart failure."

"He was murdered all right," Kildare assured them, "and the flower was placed in his hand as a little token of remembrance." He glanced at his wrist watch. "The coroner ought to be here before long," he observed.

Rod Carson who was standing last in the alley turned toward the street.

"I think that's his car now," he said.

Then two men were walking carefully down the alley behind swaying flashlights. The coroner, a stout, jovial little fellow, crowded in beside the corpse. After a look at the body of Ming Lee he chuckled.

"What do you want me for?" he asked. "Can't you tell he's dead? All fixed up with a lily in his hand, even. All he needs is a hole in the ground and some dirt and he'll be all settled."

"We want a thorough post-mortem of the body," Kildare said.

"I was afraid of that," the coroner grunted. He jerked his head toward the two men who had accompanied him. "Load him into the meat box, boys," he said, "and we'll get going."

But Kildare, Hazard, and Carson didn't join them. Instead, the government man took charge of the black lotus flower. He placed his handkerchief over the blossom and when they were out on the street once more, he gave it to one of the police officers.

"Take that to the chemical laboratory and have it analyzed for poison," he ordered.

The cops left the three of them alone in Mott Street.

CHAPTER 3
THE LIVING CORPSE

H AZARD FELT sure that a hundred eyes were watching them, as they stood in the dimly-lighted thoroughfare. He saw someone peering from an upstairs window across the street, only to vanish a moment later. What could be accomplished with Chinese eyes spying on every move they made? If they came close to Mohra's hiding place, she would be moved somewhere else until it was time for her execution.

They were walking down Pell Street, the narrowest of Chinatown's main thoroughfares. At the head of the street, Kildare stopped in a dark entrance that was shrouded from the dim street lamps.

"We'll watch from here for a while," he suggested. "We've got half an hour until midnight."

"You mean," Hazard demanded suddenly, "that we're going to stand here for that half hour? Isn't there something we can do to find Mohra?"

Hazard saw Kildare's head turn quickly in the darkness, saw his eyes rest upon him for a moment, then turn away.

"No," he said a little tensely, "there's nothing we can do about that until midnight."

While they waited, it was obvious that something was stirring beneath Chinatown. The streets were fast filling with Chinese, very unusual at that hour of the night. Furthermore the yellow men's actions seemed strange.

"I hope," Kildare ventured, "that the Chinaman who owns the shop where we're standing doesn't belong to the Chang Li. If he comes out this way, we're very apt not to see much."

Carson nudged Hazard, nodded across the street.

"Look there," he said.

For a brief moment, the figure of a man appeared. But the head on the shoulders was four times the normal size of a man's head. The figure went down a steep flight of stairs leading off the sidewalk to a basement. Two more figures came from farther down the street and vanished. Yellow men were emerging and disappearing faster and faster.

"There certainly are a lot of them," Kildare remarked.

Other figures began drifting down the street. These were white men, big and dressed in dark blue uniforms. New York police were slipping into Pell Street to be on the job for the weird parade.

The very air itself was becoming tense. There was no effort on the part of the police to stop the Chinamen who appeared. They had nothing on them, nothing to hold them for and they certainly couldn't prevent them from going on with their festive ceremonies even if it was at midnight.

Kildare glanced at his watch as lights glowed far down the street.

"The parade's forming," he said.

Hazard's teeth were clenched, his body taut. He was ready.

"Shall we go down and meet it?" he asked.

"No," Kildare said, "we'll wait. If the Chang Li parade gets this far without anything happening, they'll think they're O.K."

Hazard leaned out of the doorway and stared down. Kildare's hand was on his arm, restraining him.

"Hold everything, Jerry," he said.

"I'll—try," Hazard promised. "But we can't let this slip, Kildare."

"We're not going to," the government man said calmly. He, too, glanced down the street. Yes, the parade was forming. There was the smoke and glow of josh sticks and there were torches held high.

Then the procession moved toward them, winding its way through the narrow little street of mystery. In the lead were four yellow men, dressed alike in gorgeous, heavily-embroidered yellow robes. The false heads on their shoulders were all the same, too. They had black hair drawn back at the top and fastened in a short, stubby pigtail at the rear. But the most striking thing about the heads were their expressions, grimaced and contorted in fierce fighting scowls, as though they were meant to scare women and children.

Six men were bearing a Chinese casket, totally unlike any used in the Occidental world.

Behind the coffin was the huge dragon's head borne by two members of the Chang Li walking inside it, while the dragon's body strung out for many feet behind, supported by a long line of marchers. More yellow men with great heads marched on either side of the dragon as an escort. Weird-sounding music came from players who walked at either side of the dragon's head.

Hazard's whole attention was concentrated now on the strange oriental coffin that was moving toward them. He wondered if Kildare anticipated his intention. Probably the government man suspected the same thing he did. That the coffin didn't contain the effigy of Sun Hu Chek, but held a living body which was going to be sacrificed. And they were here now, he and Carson and Kildare, to capture it—to wrest it from the clutches of this weird, secret organization.

The first marchers with their torches and josh sticks were almost in front of their doorway. And there was the casket and the six bearers with the huge false heads. Those particular false heads had laughing expressions painted on them, showing the joy of the Chang Li in burning the effigy of the old emperor whom they had defeated long ago. The casket was almost opposite them.

Hazard's heart was pounding like mad, as though those heart beats were telling him, *"Go! Go! Go!"* He forgot that Kildare's hand was still on his arm, forgot that he was supposed to wait until the government man gave the word—forgot everything except that casket, and his certainty that Mohra was inside.

His muscles were taut. Then everything snapped and he dashed out of the doorway headlong for the casket and the six bearers. His head was down and he was charging like a football player as he raced across the sidewalk into the street.

Bang!

JERRY HAZARD'S charging body struck the two forward bearers of the coffin, hurling them to the side. Things were spinning about him pretty fast now. Hazard heard a cop yell, "Hey, stop that! What's going on?"

He spun around and charged back. Then something flashed in front of him. Another body. Two of the bearers went down and Hazard realized that Rod Carson had gone into action.

Crash!

The casket fell to the pavement and there was the sound of splintering wood. A big Chinaman loomed before Hazard, knife in his upraised hand. But the yellow man had a half-mad white adversary to deal with. Hazard never knew where he got all the strength he put behind that right fist of his, but he struck a powerful lightning fast blow full on the Chinaman's chin. The yellow man was hurled back, his knife clattered to the pavement, and he went down limp as a rag. A wild bedlam of Chinese voices rang out.

Then a voice muffled by a great head boomed out in a sing-song command. At his word, every yellow man obeyed. A reverent hush fell over the crowd, broken only by the voice of the Chinese speaker—

But Hazard whirled as he saw Kildare ripping the lid loose off the coffin and rushed over to assist. Carson was standing at the head end of the coffin with his back to it, an automatic in each hand trained on the Chinese before him.

But apparently, Carson didn't need to hold the yellow men at bay now. That authoritative voice of their chief was doing it much more effectively.

The sight that met Hazard's eyes made his heart beat wildly, raised his hopes and dashed them to the ground all in the same breath. Inside the coffin was Mohra, the dark exotic beauty whom he sought to win from the power of Wu Fang, Dragon Lord of Crime. Her lovely, dark eyes were closed as though in sleep, but her body was lying in a pitifully twisted position. It had been shoved toward the head of the long box when the casket fell.

A sudden, icy wave of fear passed over Hazard.

"Mohra!" he cried desperately. "Mohra, look at me! Tell me you're all right! Mohra darling!"

Kildare was still standing beside him. Then another figure came and stood on the other side. The man was small and wiry and dressed in the yellow robes of one of the leaders of the procession.

"Am I to understand that this lovely girl was found in the coffin instead of the effigy of Sun Hu Chek?" the voice asked.

Hazard whirled on him angrily.

"What are you trying to do, crawl out of this?" he demanded. "That would be just the kind of a trick a bird like you would pull. Secret order of Chang Li! It's nothing but a murder society. You knew very well that Mohra was in this casket. You'll hang for this, you and your yellow dogs."

But the voice of the little Chinaman replied calmly to Hazard's tirade, "I am deeply grieved, Mr. Hazard, but I think I understand more fully now. You will think better of the Chang Li when you are not so angry. Permit me to state"—and now the head raised toward Kildare—"that I am as much surprised, perhaps more so, to find this beautiful girl in the coffin. A grave mistake his been made."

The Chinaman lowered his voice as he went on, "It is an insult to the Chang Li and to our customs that have been in practice for a thousand years. Mohra, yes, that is her name. I recognize her, of course. If you will permit me, I believe I can help her regain consciousness."

The Chinese leader's hand dove into his yellow robe and brought out a tiny hypodermic needle. He raised his voice in a command and some of his yellow men brought their torches closer.

Trembling with anxiety, Hazard watched the hypodermic needle prick the white flesh of Mohra's forearm. There was a moment of suspense. The little Chinaman straightened.

"The eyes will open in a minute," he said. "The lids are fluttering like the wings of a bird."

Hazard could see that his words were true as he leaned over eagerly. The girl's head rolled a little. Then her bewildered eyes lifted to the newspaper man's face.

"You are all right, Jerry?" she asked weakly.

"Yes, of course," Hazard said quickly. "And you—are you all right?"

"Yes, dear, but I feel strange—as though I had been asleep for a long time," she answered. "Who are these other people?"

"Never mind that," Hazard said gently. "Come on. I'm going to get you out of here. Can you sit up?"

At that moment, Kildare took command. He turned to the little Chinaman who had administered the hypodermic and asked, "Will she be all right now without any further attention?"

"I am sure of it," the yellow man said.

"Then you'd better get started," Kildare told Hazard. He turned to a police officer who was standing at his elbow and ordered, "Sergeant, you'd better take three cars of men. Hazard will tell you where he and Mohra will go. Guard that girl every minute. And when I say guard her, I mean just that. I'll explain to the captain where you've gone when I get through here."

The sergeant nodded.

Kildare turned to Hazard. "Good luck," he said, "to you and Mohra both. Carson and I will carry on here."

Hazard, with Mohra moving a bit unsteadily beside him, walked a little distance to the end of the street where the police cars were parked. They climbed in, and under the heavy guard that Kildare had requested, they moved uptown.

CHAPTER 4
THE MURDER TRAIL

ROD CARSON had watched Hazard and Mohra escorted between burning torches until they rounded the corner. His automatics were in his pocket now where Kildare had ordered them. He shook his head.

"If I were in Jerry Hazard's shoes," he said, "I'd be worried sick every minute of the day and night."

"I'm worried myself," the government man confessed. "I'm afraid this is just the beginning. From now on almost anything can happen. Wu Fang isn't going to forget this very soon."

A police patrol came racing down the street. Men, yellow and white, leaped out of its way as it squealed to a stop near Kildare and Carson. More officers from the Mulberry Street station, headed by the captain, piled out and raced up to the government man. The captain squinted and blinked at him in the light of the torches that the yellow men with the great false heads were still holding.

He said nothing in that first glance at Kildare but a moment later as his eyes swept over the mass of Chinamen, he exploded, "I hope you don't think we're going to take all these Chinks down the headquarters."

Kildare smiled.

"I don't think it will be necessary to take any of them to headquarters," he said.

"Huh?" the captain demanded. "What's this I've been hearing about a human sacrifice?"

The wiry little Chinaman who had seemed to take command from the start of the trouble, spoke up from under his false head.

"We of the Chang Li thank you, Mr. Kildare," he said. "It is an honor indeed to know such a fine gentleman. You believe, then, that we are not to blame for this, that we were not aware of the body of that beautiful girl being in the coffin?"

The police captain jerked his head toward the Chinaman and demanded, "Say, who is this guy anyway?"

"I believe," the government man said, "he is the leader of the Chang Li."

"Well, what's the idea of letting him get away with the disguise? Let's find out who he is."

"No," Kildare said, shaking his head. "It wouldn't do any particular good. I can produce him any time you want him if that's what you're after."

"But look here," the captain barked.

"Wait, please," Kildare said. "I have another suggestion. You remember that I was the one who notified you about this parade coming off. Now I'm asking you in the name of common sense to let them finish their celebration. And not only that, but"— Kildare's voice lowered and he leaned closer to the captain's ear—"you'll be helping out a lot if you order your men back to Mulberry Street."

"Well, of all the things that could happen," the captain burst out. "First you come running to me and tell me there's going to be a parade and I'd better have the boys out to keep order and now—"

He broke off and shook his head disgustedly. Then he jerked his head toward the waiting police and dismissed them.

When they had gone, the little Chinaman bowed jerkily to Kildare.

"You will excuse us now?" he asked. "We will go to the other end of the street and form the parade again."

"That will be all right," Kildare assured him. "Go ahead."

But Kildare was not so sure. He walked thoughtfully around the corner with Carson.

"What do we do now?" the young explorer asked. "Run out on them?"

"Hardly," Kildare smiled. "I'm not too sure of things yet. There's something funny going on here."

"I'd like to ride this thing through to the finish," Carson said suddenly. "Mohra in the coffin coupled up with the murder of Ming Lee and the black lotus—"

He shook his head perplexedly.

"I WOULDN'T trust that gang any further than I could throw an elephant," he finished.

"I don't know," Kildare said. "That's one of the things we've got to find out for certain. But there's one member of the Chang Li that I'm going to get if it's humanly possible."

40

"Meaning Wu Fang, of course," Carson suggested.

"Yes," Kildare admitted. "Wu Fang was in that parade tonight. I'm sure of it."

In the middle of the back street, he and Carson entered an alley.

"I hope," Carson ventured, "that you know where you're going."

"I do," Kildare nodded. "It's pretty dark and smelly in here but we'll come out on Pell Street again."

"Oh, I get it," Carson said. "We're going to hide there and watch the parade go by again."

"And that's not all," Kildare said. "We're not just going to watch the parade; we're going to try and find out just where certain things break up. I wish we had a couple of those costumes and heads."

Carson grinned and his eyes flashed.

"I'll get you a couple if you want them, Kildare," he offered.

But Kildare knew how he would obtain them. There would be a slam-bang-biff row and Carson would come running back with the necessary adornments, in which case there would be several Chinamen lying in the street. So the government man shook his head in the negative as they crossed a tiny back yard into another alley.

"I'd like to have the costumes and heads for a disguise," he said, "but I'm afraid the way you'd get them they wouldn't be much good to us."

"O.K.," Carson said, "but just what is the object of our watching the parade go by then?"

The coffin fell to the groundin the wild and sudden confusion.

He saw Kildare stop before him at the end of the alley and peer out and down the street.

"They're forming again," the government man said in a low whisper. "Now, here's what I have in mind. There's just room for two of us to stand back in this alley and cover the street fairly well. I believe we're right at the point where the parade will eventually break up. We may find all the members of the Chang Li going for one basement entrance or they may—and this is most likely I think—scurry away into various buildings like a bunch of rats running for their holes."

"You mean you're going to follow them?" Carson cried eagerly.

"That's the idea I have in mind," Kildare admitted. "But I want to follow the right parties. I think I know that little Chinaman who appears to be the leader of the Chang Li. Here they come now." Carson heard the whine of the off-key oriental music, heard the shuffle of the feet. He moved out a little farther so that he could look down the street.

Kildare pointed to the man on the left of the four leaders with their ugly, grimacing faces.

"There he is," the government man said. "The little fellow on the left."

"I see him," Carson whispered. "When this breaks up, we're going to try to trail him," Kildare added. "But remember, no disturbance."

The second edition of the parade of the Chang Li came on. Rod Carson felt Kildare's hand rest on his arm as the four leaders of the procession passed them. Now came the casket.

Kildare hissed in Carson's ear, "We're going to make sure of what's in that casket before—"

The government man's words ceased as though they had been cut off with an axe as a Chinaman came down the street.

The six bearers were carrying the queer-shaped coffin. Carson knew it was the same casket that had been used before for he could see the scratches on it where Kildare had torn it open.

Kildare's hand gripped Carson's wrist.

"Tell me when the lights go out," he ordered.

"Tell you?" Carson burst out. "Can't you see for yourself?"

He turned now, and he saw that Kildare had his eyes closed.

"What's the idea?" he demanded.

"I'll talk until the torches are blown out," Kildare said. "The minute they go out, interrupt me. Those torches are blinding; they form strange shadows. I'm working on a hunch that when the lights are extinguished, the members of the Chang Li will scatter in all directions. I want you to keep your eyes on the little Chinese leader up front. I'm keeping my eyes closed so that they will be accustomed to the darkness when the lights go out. There! I hear something now."

THE SAME sound came to Carson's ears. A deep-throated Chinese voice. The largest of the four leaders was shouting a command in Cantonese. Although Carson couldn't understand a word, he knew that the command was a signal to the torch bearers. As the big fellow finished his command, he brandished his own torch through the air and it went out. A concentrated movement of torches followed.

"They're out!" Carson cried. "Great Scott, it's as dark as pitch!"

"Come on!" Kildare hissed. "Did you see which way the leader went?"

"To the right, I think," Carson said. "To the other side of the street. I can see a bunch of figures over there, but I can't distinguish any of them."

"I can see pretty well," Kildare said. "Let's get on the other side of the street and keep an eye on that leader."

The members of the Chang Li were fleeing. And, as Kildare had guessed, they were all rushing toward various doorways and staircases leading down off the street.

They took no notice of Kildare or Carson. Perhaps they, too, were partially blinded from the sudden extinction of the torches. A light odor of incense hung about the air.

"I never saw a crowd of people vanish so quickly," Carson said as he reached the center of the deserted street. "There isn't a soul left. Where did that dragon and casket go?"

"Never mind," Kildare cried sharply. "Come on! Hurry!"

Suddenly, he slowed his pace.

"I've got it," he said. "Now, let's take our time."

"Got what?" Carson demanded.

"The place," Kildare hissed, "where our little Chinese leader disappeared. I just managed to catch sight of him as he was going through the door."

Kildare jerked his head toward a steep, very narrow stairs that led abruptly off the sidewalk.

Kildare led the way down the stairs, squeezing through the passage. There was a muffled jangling of keys as he reached the bottom.

"There," Kildare said at length, replacing the skeleton keys in his pocket.

"Put your hand on my shoulder," Kildare whispered. "I don't want to use a light. Got to feel my way. You follow."

"Right," Carson agreed.

Step by step they advanced. Then Kildare stopped.

"Another door," he whispered.

Then Carson heard a strange sound, a soft but ominous tapping that seemed to fill the room like the muffled beating of a drum.

"I have it," Kildare said softly.

Carson still had his hand on the government man's shoulder. Suddenly, he felt Kildare drop out from under it.

CHAPTER 5
THE TEMPLE OF CHANG LI

KILDARE WAS bending over. There came a soft, groaning sound.

"Come on," he whispered.

And then Carson knew what had happened. The government man had found a trap door in the floor. As they descended a flight of very steep stairs, Carson noticed that the odor of age and dampness was stronger than ever.

Step by step they continued downward.

"I don't think these steps are ever going to end," Kildare whispered.

But at length they did reach the bottom.

"Phew!" Carson whistled, "that's the longest bunch of steps I ever went down when I couldn't see where I was going. Know how many there were, Kildare?"

"Yes," the government man said. "I counted them. Sixty three."

Once more Carson had his hand on Kildare's shoulder as they proceeded along the narrow corridor. Suddenly, the government man stopped, stopped so suddenly that Carson at once sensed danger.

"That's funny," he heard Kildare say. "We seem to be at the end of our rope or rather at the end of our alley. This corridor stops here."

"What?" Carson gasped.

"That's right. Feel for yourself."

The two men stood motionless for a moment, as a dull sound filled the long chamber. The very air about them seemed to shudder.

Then, as though it were a trick to startle them, from far off came the sound of a gong, deep, mellow, vibrant.

"Where did that sound come from?" Kildare asked, turning to Carson.

"I'm not sure," the young explorer replied, "but I think it came from somewhere not far off. We heard it through these walls."

Now Carson could smell a familiar odor common to the Orient.

"There's one sure thing," he said. "That incense smell isn't coming down that flight of sixty-three steps. Incense smoke travels upward or at least laterally, but never down."

"Have you heard anything from the direction of the stairs?" Kildare whispered.

"No," Carson answered. "Not a sound."

"Very well," Kildare said. "I'll turn on my flash and we'll go to work on this incense smoke."

His light streamed down the passage, and as though that had been a signal, the great gong sounded again.

"Where's that sound coming from and what does it mean?" Carson hissed.

"With luck," Kildare said, "we'll be in the temple of the Chang Li before very long. I think the gong is coming from there and the smell of incense as well."

Kildare dropped the light beam to the floor of the passage.

"I'll stand here at this end, Carson," he said. "You walk slowly down toward the bottom of the stairs. Breathe not too deeply but rather rapidly. Get what I mean? When you come back, tell me where you think the incense odor is the strongest."

Carson did as Kildare ordered. He was used to tunnels and passages and the weird, strange things of other lands, but nevertheless, it gave him a queer sensation now as he tip-toed through the dark, foreboding passage, trying not to make a sound for fear that at any moment someone might hear him.

He sniffed the air, taking short, gentle but rapid breaths. A little distance from Kildare, he detected the strongest odor of incense.

HE REACHED the bottom of the stairs, looked up into a

black void. He turned and came back. Yes, that was the place. He told Kildare and together they strode forward.

Suddenly, Kildare stopped and crouched down low beside the wall at his right. He placed the flash light close to the wall so that the beam traveled up the side of the cut stone.

Carson saw a thin wisp of smoke coming through an even crack in the stone wall that ran up about three feet from the floor. It was in a straight line as though it had been cut purposely and still it fitted the stone next to it so perfectly that it was well hidden.

"That's clever," Kildare remarked. "We never would have found it if it hadn't been for the incense smoke."

Carson stood at the side, letting Kildare work it out. He saw the government man tracing a rough line with his finger. His hand moved to the right perhaps two feet from the straight vertical line of the cut in the rock. Then it began traveling down again toward the floor. But here the line was irregular.

Bending down, Carson saw that there was a line at the bottom of that stone section also. Kildare pushed, gently at first. Nothing happened. He pushed harder with both hands.

"It's moving!" Carson whispered excitedly. "I can see it. Wait, let me give you a hand."

They braced themselves and pushed. The slab of stone swung back into the wall. Kildare was first to crawl through the small opening.

"It looks like we're pretty close to where we're heading," Carson hissed.

"Sssh!" Kildare cautioned. "Take it easy. Listen!"

They crouched there, studying what lay before them. They were in a vaulted cave or temple that was carved out of the rock like the passage. The walls rose up above them for perhaps fifteen feet—then sloped away. Directly in front of them, not ten feet off, was a screen of heavy tapestries.

From beyond those drapes, the sound of voices came to them, but neither Carson nor Kildare could catch the meaning of the words spoken in Cantonese. Judging from the tone of the voice that was speaking, Carson guessed that the speaker was very angry.

Suddenly, he felt Kildare tense and reach for his gun.

"Come on," the government man hissed. "I recognize that voice. Do you know who it is?"

Carson shook his head.

"I do," Kildare snapped. "It's the one man in the world that I'm after." With that, Kildare sprang straight for a break in the tapestries. Carson jerked out his two automatics and together they burst through the curtain.

The sight that met their eyes was awe-inspiring, to say the least. Apparently they had entered the temple of the Chang Li through the secret passage meant only for the high governors who now stood on the back of a raised platform which was carpeted with rich oriental rugs. Evidently, this was the alter upon which sacrifices were made.

Just ahead of them were the backs of the four yellow men, the leaders of the grotesque procession that had a little time before wound its way through Pell Street.

There were the three larger men who seemed to be in the

Kildare and Carson burst through the screen.

background of the altar platform. Before them stood the little commanding Chinaman, before whom was the casket that had been carried in the parade. Beneath it, wood and kindling were piled in a heap, ready to be ignited for the sacrifice.

But neither the coffin nor the altar itself was holding the attention of the members of the Chang Li. Instead, every eye was focused on a tall, narrow-shouldered, gaunt Chinaman at a door at the back of the temple.

Carson and Kildare realized that it had apparently been this Chinaman whose voice they had heard addressing the assembled members of the Chang Li. As they burst through the curtain, he turned and the door swung shut on him.

But that didn't stop Kildare. The government man's automatic was up and he was dashing forward across the altar platform, pulling the trigger as fast as he could. Wood splintered from the back door of the temple.

Kildare and Carson reached the rear door of the temple together. As they burst through, they heard a grinding sound out beyond.

Bam!

They came up against a stone wall four feet ahead. Kildare swung to the right, Carson to the left. But stone walls met them on every side. This was no exit, and yet Wu Fang had fled this way.

Carson spun around and plunged back into the solid rock temple. His two guns were leveled at the little figure on the platform far down front.

"Pull the lever that opens that blank wall or I'll blast you into the hottest place in the universe," he yelled.

The little Chinese leader seemed not the least perturbed as he answered, "You shall have all the aid at our command."

He turned and spoke rapidly in Cantonese, while a half dozen members of the Chang Li turned their great false heads and leaped to their feet about Carson.

The young explorer's guns moved, but the little figure on the platform warned quickly, "Do not shoot these men. They are carrying out your orders."

Carson was standing at the door, holding it open. The six members of the Chang Li went out into the hall. Carson couldn't see what was done but he guessed that they must have pushed a hidden button or an unnoticed lever. The wall at the back swung away like a great door, revealing a passageway that led to the top of a flight of stairs.

Kildare snapped on his flash light and raced down the stairs three steps at a time. At the bottom, he stopped suddenly. A labyrinth of passages all leading in different directions met his eyes.

"**WHICH WAY** did Wu Fang go?" he demanded, whirling to the yellow men who had trailed them.

All six shook their great heads. A big fellow spoke in a deep, cultured voice.

"We do not know," he said. "He has gone, but we can not tell which way."

The speaker stretched out his long arm, extended his long-nailed fingers in a sweeping gesture toward the various passages.

"There could be perhaps three hundred places where these passages lead," he said. "We know Wu Fang well. You could search two hundred and ninety-nine of them and he would be in the three hundredth. I assure you it would be futile for you to continue."

For a long moment, Kildare studied those passages. Carson looked at the floors of the various corridors. There was no way in which they could tell the passing of Wu Fang. Many feet had recently trod these stone corridors. At length, Kildare shrugged.

"That was close," he said. "But next time we will have to do better than that." He turned. "And now," he said, "I think we have a little business upstairs in the temple of Chang Li."

They climbed the stairs again to the temple.

Then the government man was saying to the commanding little figure, "You are sure now that the casket contains no human being?"

The leader bowed.

"I am very positive," he said, "but in order to prove it to you, and to repay your kindness to the members of the Chang Li, I will show you. You will come up beside the altar, please, honorable sir."

Kildare and Carson stepped up on the raised platform. There came the sound of nails squealing as the little Chinese commander forced open the lid of the casket. The two men bent down and looked in. There was a figure inside the coffin but when Kildare poked it with his hand, it rustled. This time it was an effigy of the emperor Sun Hu Chek made of clothing and stuffed with straw.

"You are quite satisfied?" the leader asked.

"Yes," Kildare nodded. "Quite."

The little Chinaman hesitated, then continued, "And are you entirely convinced that we did not block your way when you pursued Wu Fang?"

"It's quite all right," Kildare assured him.

"Then if we have your permission and your blessing, honorable Mr. Kildare and of your friend"—he bowed to Carson—"We will escort you out of the temple and proceed with the ceremony."

"Very well," Kildare agreed. "How do we go?"

"If you please, honorable gentlemen," the leader said, "you will go separately. Our order is secret, our temple is secret. I realize now how you found your way in. It was through the carelessness of myself and the other three governors. But rest assured that that passage will be closed up definitely. You will be the last to use it. You, Mr. Kildare and your friend will be blind-folded—then you will be led out separate ways. You may arrange a meeting place."

"Say look here," Carson exploded, "what's the idea of splitting us?"

"If you please, honorable sir," the little Chinaman begged, "we cast no reflections upon you gentlemen whatsoever. It is merely that we must do everything possible to preserve our secrecy. Too many secrets have already been given out."

"Yes." Kildare nodded, "I'm going to ask you some questions about that tomorrow perhaps."

"Tomorrow?" the little man repeated. "Oh, yes, I understand." Then to Carson he explained, "We are conducting you out of here by two different routes simply so you will not be able to compare your experience and solve the secret of entrance. We do not wish any who are not members of the Chang Li to return. But rest assured this is no trick. You will be perfectly safe."

"You'll be all right, Carson," Kildare assured him. "I'd stake my life on it. I'll meet you at the Mulberry Street police station." He nodded to the little Chinaman. "Very well," he said, "blindfold us and start us on our way."

Darkness closed in on Rod Carson when they placed the bandage over his eyes. Then two men were leading him, one by each arm. After what seemed hours had passed, he was left standing on a sidewalk.

A voice said, "You may take off the blind now."

Carson blinked and stared about him. He was in an alley. That was all he knew except that there was more light above at the top of the buildings that flanked him on either side than anywhere else. He started down the alley, but came to a dead end.

As he turned back, he heard a sound behind him. He stopped to listen, dropped his hands to his guns. He didn't trust that Chang Li bunch. Yes, something had moved down there where he had been a moment before. He drew his guns.

His mind was a tangle of confused plans and decisions. One

moment he was definitely going to call out and warn whoever had been moving to stop or he would shoot. The next instant he realized that anyone might have a right in this mass of back alleys.

Suddenly a voice came to him out of the darkness at his right, very soft and low.

"Mr. Rod Carson."

CHAPTER 6
MESSENGER OF DEATH

ROD CARSON spun half around as though he were on a turn-table, his two automatics whirling with him. Now he saw a figure not five feet away, coming toward him, nearer and nearer.

He heard that lovely, soothing voice, tinged ever so slightly with the accent of a foreign tongue.

"Please, Mr. Rod Carson," it pleaded, "put your guns away. They are not necessary, I assure you."

At the same time, two soft hands reached out and rested on his wrists, gently pushing the guns down.

The speaker was very close to him, and in spite of the darkness, he could see that she was tall, graceful and very beautiful.

"You recognize me, perhaps?" she asked. "You remember Tanya?"

Rod Carson drew himself up to his full height.

"Yes," he said stiffly, "I remember you, Tanya. Could anyone forget your treachery? Do you think you're going to trick me again?"

Tanya's voice was tender as she answered, "I am very sorry, Mr. Carson. How sorry, I cannot tell you. I admit it is true that I helped Wu Fang capture you and Mr. Hazard, but there are reasons. I have not time to tell you them now, but perhaps some day you will understand."

Suddenly, Carson felt her hand resting on his arm as she pleaded. "Please do not think too harshly of me. Some day you will know the truth. But for now, I can only tell you that I come as a messenger from Wu Fang. And what I have for you, will, I believe, make you think more kindly of my master."

"Your master!" Carson repeated, stepping back. "Do you mean to say that Wu Fang is your master, Tanya? You admit it? Great Scott, what are you thinking of? Do you work with him willingly?"

The beautiful blonde girl before him stiffened, held herself proudly erect.

"I have told you before," she said, "there are some things you will some day understand. But for the present, Wu Fang is my master. That is enough."

As the girl drew back from Carson, he reached out to catch her arm. As she took another step backward, her hand was in Carson's for a moment.

Carson closed his hand quickly, but only over a folded slip of paper. He lunged forward, groping in the darkness. But Tanya was gone.

After several futile attempts, Rod Carson succeeded in lighting a match and holding it up. In the dim flickering light, he stared about hopelessly trying to locate Tanya.

A puff of wind snuffed out the match. He lighted another, shielding the flame as he held it over the slip of paper. The message was short and easily legible. It said:

> BE ADVISED THAT TONIGHT THE CHANG LI
> WILL KILL AT THE HOME OF JUSTIN BROCK.
> WU FANG.

Tonight! Why, that would mean this morning. Yes, it was morning now. Justin Brock. Who was that?

Carson stood there for a moment, baffled. Which way would lead him out?

Suddenly he heard a voice to the left and behind him. It was little more than a whisper but it carried to him easily and he knew it was the voice of Tanya, the lovely, blonde siren who had trapped Hazard and him once in the canyons of the West. And she was calling to him now, very softly.

"Which way, Tanya?" he called softly.

"Follow my voice," the girl replied.

And now the sound was muffled, but the direction was very definite. Carson had turned and was running up another dark alley.

"Wait, Tanya," he called.

But the girl answered, "Follow my voice," and she was as far ahead of him now as when he had first heard her.

Rod Carson stopped short and listened.

Again he heard her say, "Follow my voice."

This time she was still farther away. Evidently she hadn't stopped when he did. He began running once more. Suddenly, he stopped again as his outstretched hands struck a blank wall.

Then the voice of the girl said, "This way."

He called softly, "Wait, Tanya. Who is this Justin Brock that's mentioned in the note?"

But it was as though Tanya had suddenly evaporated into thin air. Her voice came no more.

Rod Carson walked down that alley a distance of perhaps fifty feet until he suddenly found himself on the sidewalk of one of Chinatown's narrow streets. He strode on up to the corner where Mott Street crossed it.

Now that he was out in the open on a street corner with a dim light burning above him, what he had just been through seemed almost unbelievable.

But Carson didn't take time to ponder those things. He was running across and down that next narrow thoroughfare of Chinatown toward the Mulberry Street police station where he was to meet Kildare.

He charged up the steps of the station and asked the first officer he saw, "Has Kildare come yet?"

The cop looked at him peculiarly.

"Kildare?" he repeated. "Sure and what would he be coming here for? Are we supposed to be looking for him?"

"He said he'd meet me here," Carson explained.

"Well, then, he'll probably be along."

But Carson wasn't so sure of that and time was precious.

The officer at the desk motioned him to a bench.

"Sit down and take it easy," he advised. "What's on your mind?"

CARSON HESITATED. There was plenty on his mind—Justin Brock and the murder that was to be committed at his house tonight. Word should be sent to the Brock house at once.

Five minutes went by but it seemed an hour to Carson. He couldn't wait any longer for Kildare. Anyway, why shouldn't the police know about the note he had received? He took it out and walked over to the officer at the desk. The sergeant glanced at it, his eyes widening.

"Suffering catfish!" the desk sergeant exclaimed. "Where did you get this?"

"It was handed to me in Chinatown," Carson told him. "A girl gave it to me and disappeared."

"Didn't you try to follow her?" the sergeant demanded. "I'll bet she was going right back to Wu Fang."

"Follow her?" Carson repeated. "I didn't have a chance."

"Well, I'd like to see a girl get away from me if I didn't want her to," the sergeant grunted. Then he raised his voice and shouted, "Hey, you boys!"

He was directing his orders toward some plain clothes men who were at the moment absorbed in a card game. "Jump in the wagon and go up to Justin Brock's place. We've just got a tip that there's murder coming off there tonight."

"Justin Brock's place?" one of the detectives demanded, getting up.

"Right," the desk sergeant nodded. "You know where he lives?"

"Sure do," the detective nodded. "What are they going to commit murder up there about?"

"Who is this Justin Brock?" Rod Carson demanded.

The sergeant turned to one of the detectives.

"Tell him who Brock is," he ordered.

"He's a publisher," the detective said.

"A publisher?" Carson repeated.

"Yes. A big shot in his line. Can't figure why they want to bump him off. That Chang Li outfit is liable to do anything."

"Maybe," the desk sergeant said. "And again maybe somebody has got scared because they heard some talking."

The phone on his desk demanded attention. He picked it up.

"Hello. Yeah. What?… Oh, good evening, Mr. Danowski. What did you say?… Yes, sir. Right away. Got a squad of the best men here now. They're just going out. They'll stop and have a look at things on their way. Yes, sir."

The sergeant hung up the receiver and called to the plain clothes men who were half way to the outer door.

"Hey, you, Johnny Danowski, the political boss of mid Manhattan just called to say he's got a little matter for you to take care of. Stop on your way up to Brock's place. And do what he wants, see—if you want to hold your jobs."

The detectives nodded and went on.

Carson whirled and stared in astonishment at the desk sergeant.

"You mean?" he demanded, "that you're delaying these men on their way to Brock's place?"

The sergeant shrugged.

"Sure. They'll get to Brock's in time. Besides, got to take care of the big boys. I don't think this murder story is anything more than a scare anyway. Brock's place is pretty well barred up, you can be sure."

Carson leaped half way across the desk.

"Say, look here," he cried. "I've got a good notion to—"

A firm hand caught him by the shoulder from behind and pulled him back again. Carson whirled around to see Kildare.

"What's going on," Kildare demanded.

Carson told him in a few words, none of them complimentary to the now red-faced desk sergeant.

"Good," Kildare said. "I hope Danowski, or whatever his name is, keeps them there the rest of the night. They'll only mess things up if we don't beat them to it. Justin Brock's place is away uptown, and I imagine the subway express is as fast a way as any. Let's go."

They dove into the underground station just in time to slip through the closing doors of an uptown express.

"Who is this Justin Brock?" Carson demanded.

"You remember," Kildare reminded him, "that Jerry Hazard told us about that article written by Ming Lee that he had read in the Weekly post?"

Carson nodded.

"Well," Kildare went on, "Brock is the publisher of the Weekly Post."

Val Kildare and Rod Carson did beat the car of detectives to the Justin Brock mansion by quite some minutes. Kildare pushed his way past the sleepy-eyed butler who opened the door.

"Call Mr. Justin Brock at once," he ordered.

"Oh, but I say, sir," the butler protested. "The hour, sir, it's—"

Kildare flashed his badge and immediately the butler blinked and backed away.

"It's a matter of life and death," Kildare snapped.

"Yes, sir," the butler quavered. "I'll tell Mr. Brock you're waiting."

"Just a minute," Kildare said. "Is there any other member of the household, either in or outside the house tonight?"

"There's Mr. Brock, Junior. Er"—the butler glanced significantly at a clock—"he's out rather late tonight."

"He has a key to the front door?" Kildare asked.

"I believe so, although I am usually up to let him in," the butler answered.

Carson saw Kildare scrutinize the butler closely.

"Are there any other guests or friends living in the house?" he asked quickly.

The butler shook his head.

"No, sir," he said. "That is—oh, yes! There is a Mr. Schuyler here, sir. He is a friend of Mr. Brock."

"Very well. Call him too, then."

AS HE spoke, Carson heard a sound at the top of the stairs. He turned and stared up toward the landing. A heavy-set, powerful man was coming down the stairs.

"Oh, yes, sir," the butler said, turning quickly. "This is Mr. Schuyler, the gentleman I was just telling you about."

Schuyler was frowning at Carson and Kildare as he came down tire steps. He wore a bathrobe under which the legs of his pajamas showed. His feet were encased in slippers.

"What's wanted?" he demanded.

"Begging your pardon, sir," the butler announced, "but this gentleman," he nodded toward Kildare, "is a government man. I was just about to call Mr. Brock, sir."

"A government man?" Schuyler said, opening his eyes in surprise. "Is there something wrong?"

"That's what we came to find out," Kildare said, advancing.

Carson stayed where he was in the center of the great hall. He watched Kildare meet Schuyler at the bottom of the stairs.

"I'm afraid there is something wrong," Kildare said. "We received word that the Chang Li—that's a secret Chinese order—is planning a murder here at the Brock house tonight. I presume it's in retaliation for the printing of that article, on the secrets of the Chang Li, that will appear in the new issue of the Weekly Post tomorrow."

Schuyler's eyes blazed.

"Murder!" he exploded. "Good Heavens! In this house?"

"Yes," Kildare nodded. He turned to the butler. "If you don't mind, will you call Mr. Brock at once?" he asked.

Schuyler gave a sudden, nervous laugh.

"But this is rather strange, isn't it?" he asked. "I mean everything connected with tonight or this morning, rather. For some reason, I haven't been able to sleep a wink. That's why I was up and about when I heard the front door open. I thought perhaps it was young Roger Brock just getting in. That's Mr. Brock's son, you know."

The butler passed them, moving up the stairs as rapidly as his dignity would permit.

"You have known Mr. Brock and his son for some time?" Kildare asked. "The butler tells me you are an old friend."

"I haven't seen Justin for a number of years," Schuyler admitted. "We used to be great friends, but then my business kept me elsewhere. I have just returned from abroad. Tonight was our first meeting in a long tune. We're looking forward to some good long chats together."

Carson raised his eyes to the top of the great staircase as he heard a sputtering sound above. A portly, gray-haired gentleman appeared. He too, was in his bathrobe and pajamas. He blinked his eyes again and again as he came down the stairs. It was plainly evident that he had just awakened from a sound sleep.

"What is this?" he demanded. "What's going on?"

His eyes shifted from Schuyler to Kildare, then on to Carson and back to Schuyler again. Schuyler opened his mouth to speak, but Kildare cut in first.

"We are very sorry, Mr. Brock," he explained, "to trouble you at this hour. Something very important has come up, and we felt that you should not only be warned but protected as well."

Brock's eyes shifted quickly in a strange look at Schuyler. His lips tightened and his teeth clenched. The pink ruddiness of his complexion gave way to a chalky white.

"What have you heard?" he demanded. He turned quickly to the butler. "Has Roger come in yet, Tompkins?" he asked.

"No, sir," the butler bowed.

The elder Brock bit his lip.

"I'm quite sure your son will be all right," Kildare comforted, taking command of the situation. "Shall we go into the library where we can be more comfortable?"

Justin Brock was nervous and confused. He didn't answer Kildare for a moment, then he roused himself and glanced toward the library, nodding dully.

"Yes, yes, of course," he said. "Let's go into the library."

Then he himself led the way. Carson was last in that procession of four to pass into the library. He saw Kildare glance at his watch as they sat down and he knew the reason. It wouldn't be long before a carload of cops would be pulling up and running all over the place.

Suddenly, they heard a sound in the hall at the front door. Schuyler moved quickly. He was on his feet just as Brock said, "Thank heaven, that's Roger now." He started to rise but Schuyler laid a restraining hand on his shoulder.

"Don't bother," he said, "I'll let him in." He smiled at Kildare and Carson. "Sometimes," he said, "it's better if the father doesn't meet his son when he comes in at three in the morning."

Carson watched him as he turned toward the hall and went out. The library was silent, and Brock was obviously waiting for the assurance of his son's voice to tell him that he was safe. There was the sound of the great door opening.

"Hello, Roger," they heard Schuyler say. "Believe me, we're glad to see you."

Then there was another sound, so strange and startling that

all three men in the library leaped to their feet. They heard young Roger Brock say "Hello." He started to say something else, but his words changed to a shrill scream and choked off at the end in a husky sob. There was the sound of a body crashing to the floor.

CHAPTER 7
THE PHANTOM DEATH

THEY HEARD Schuyler's excited voice, and now he was running up the hall toward the library, gasping and uttering incoherent words of astonishment and surprise. Kildare and Carson followed closely as the elder Brock raced out of the library and collided with Schuyler at the entrance.

"Good heavens!" Schuyler cried. "It's Roger! I think he's dead. I don't know what happened to him. He—"

The body of a young man was stretched out in the hall. It was lying sidewise in a twisted heap, the legs across the threshold so that the door couldn't be closed without moving the body.

But it wasn't the still form of young Brock that drew the gasps of astonishment from Carson and Kildare. It was something that lay across the body. Something that had a long, green stem topped by a beautiful, black, waxy blossom.

"Good heavens!" Schuyler cried, "Where did that come from?"

Carson was just behind Kildare as the government man raced toward the body, but he didn't stop there. Carson saw the automatic leap out of his pocket, and then he was vaulting over the body and out into the darkness. Carson plunged after him.

Behind them, they could hear the elder Brock repeating over and over again in an agonized voice, "Roger! Roger, look at me! Open your eyes and tell me that you're all right!"

Schuyler's voice came faintly, trying to console the bereaved father.

The Brock mansion was one of those large, uptown residences that occupied a quarter of a block. It was set on a corner, and except for a narrow little strip of grass along the front and sides, the walls came down to the edge of the sidewalk. There was a spiked iron railing separating those grassy strips from the street, and it curved up on either side of the front entrance, so that it would be difficult for anyone to climb over it and drop onto the narrow lawn.

Kildare cleared the steps in one wild leap and landed on the sidewalk. We motioned Carson down to the left.

"You take that side and I'll take this one," he said. "Go all the way around the block and stop anyone or anything you see."

Then they were off in a wild race. As Carson charged around the next corner, he saw that the street was deserted except for one, lone cruising taxi. He raced on until he met Kildare at the other side of the block.

"Find anything?" he breathed.

"No," Kildare said. "Keep going. I'll meet you at the front of the house."

Their search was futile, and when they reached the steps to the front entrance of the Brock mansion, a police car squealed

Kildare stared at the two bodies.

to a stop at the curb. Detectives piled out and stared at Carson and Kildare.

"I suppose," said one detective, "you've got everything solved by now."

"No," Kildare said in a low voice, "but we've got something to work on. There's been one murder committed in the last five minutes."

The four detectives turned suddenly as one man and ran up the steps to the open door.

The butler, still clothed, was in the hall now, white-faced and frightened. The detectives had just made an examination of the body and pronounced young Brock dead. Now they ran up and cornered Tompkins and shot questions at him in a rapid-fire barrage. Kildare stared at the butler for a moment. Then he shook his head.

"Poor fellow," he said. "When they get through with him, they'll be sure he killed Roger Brock."

The other two detectives were interrogating Schuyler and the elder Brock. Kildare stepped over the body and went inside, but Carson remained outdoors and listened to the questioning of Schuyler. He heard him repeat his story twice, just as it had happened. He had gone to the front door, opened it, and young Roger Brock had recognized him.

"Then," he continued, "Brock said 'Hello.' He was going to speak my name, I'm sure, but there was no time. He cried out and toppled to the floor. Of course, I was horrified; I didn't know what I was doing. I can't remember just what did happen then, but as I recall, the two gentlemen who came here to warn

Mr. Brock were in the library. I ran back to get them and met them at the door. When I turned to point to Roger's body, there was the black flower on it."

"Say," cried one of the detectives, "that black what-you-may-call-it is the sacred flower of the Chang Li. That Chink Ming Lee had one pinned on him when he was found dead last night."

"Yes," Kildare nodded. "That's the black lotus. Apparently, it's a sign."

"You're right, it's a sign," one of the detectives cut in. "It's a sign that the Chang Li did the job."

Kildare shot a significant glance over the heads of the others at Carson and winked.

"Yes," he said, "I think it would be a good idea if the Chang Li organization were rounded up and held under suspicion."

The detective nearest glared at him.

"Oh, yeh?" he growled. "Well, maybe, we would have rounded up the whole gang at the parade tonight, if you hadn't talked the chief into letting them pitch another party. And now look what you've got us into. It looks as though this is just the start of a whole series of murders."

"That's right," Kildare admitted. "I hadn't thought of that." HE WINKED again at Carson and nodded significantly toward the library. He crossed the hall so that he and Carson met where Schuyler and Mr. Brock were being questioned. They waited a moment while the detective questioned Schuyler. "How do you account for that black lotus in there?"

"I don't know how it got there," Schuyler said, shaking his head. "It wasn't there when I ran to tell the others in the library."

"When you're through with Mr. Schuyler," Kildare said, "I'd like to talk over some things with him to get the story straight."

"O.K.," the detective shrugged. "He's yours."

"Of course," Kildare reminded them, "we were in the library when it happened. I formed my own general construction of the happenings but I may be wrong. I'd like to have Schuyler's version, since he was there."

"Indeed, you shall have it," Schuyler said.

Justin Brock took one look at the body of his son on the floor.

"Perhaps you'd be more comfortable in the library, Mr. Brock," Kildare suggested.

The white-haired publisher nodded. Kildare saw that the grief was almost more than he could bear.

"Just a minute, Mr. Schuyler," the government man said. "Will you give me a hand with young Brock's body?"

Justin Brock had passed through the door into the library. Schuyler bent down stiffly, but straightened again with one hand at his back.

"I'm afraid I must refuse," he said.

At that, Carson stepped forward and he and Kildare lifted Roger Brock's body and carried it just inside the hall. They were careful to lay it down in exactly the same position it had been in before. Then Kildare closed the front door.

Schuyler was standing with both hands at his back now, bending over. His face was contorted a little with pain.

"I had a bad attack of lumbago," he explained. "I forgot about it for the moment. My back gives me a twinge every time I bend over. But to go on with my story, I—"

"Just a moment," Kildare interrupted. "Before we go on with the story, I'd like to make a suggestion. It wouldn't do any harm, you know, if the house were searched thoroughly."

He looked down at the still form on the floor. There was no sign of blood visible—no prick of a poison dart at the back of his neck.

A moment later, all four detectives had disappeared into various parts of the mansion. The butler still remained at the back of the hall.

"You see," Schuyler explained, drawing his bathrobe a little tighter about him, "I couldn't swear as to how Roger was killed. He just keeled over, that was all."

"Where were you standing?" Kildare asked, "when you let him in the door?"

Schuyler seemed to ponder for a moment. He stepped toward the door.

"Let's see," he said. "I came before the door like this." He demonstrated his words. "Then I opened it, of course, and stepped aside, as the door swung inward."

Kildare walked over in front of the door now. Schuyler hadn't actually opened the door; he had merely made the motions to illustrate his words. The government man seemed to be lining up the opening of the door with the stairs at the other side of the hall and also with other objects—a carved table, the crook in the staircase, and a great, spangled chandelier that hung from the ceiling.

"Then as you stood aside, Schuyler," he said, "something, perhaps a poison dart, might have been blown from the staircase, or from beneath that stand, or from the chandelier above?"

Schuyler surveyed the stairs and the rear of the hall and the other fixtures that Kildare had mentioned. He nodded slowly.

"Yes," he said. "I'd say that it would have been possible. But then, on the other hand, it might have come from outdoors. In all probability, it did, as I come to think of it now."

"What makes you believe that?" Kildare asked.

Schuyler shrugged and pointed to the black lotus flower beside the body.

"How did that get there?" he asked. "It certainly wasn't there when Roger fell, almost into my arms. I turned and ran back to the library door and when I returned it was there, and of course, you know the front door was open."

Kildare nodded to Carson.

"Take a look out the back of the hall, Carson," he suggested. "Search the back of the house thoroughly. I'm going in and see what I can do to console Mr. Brock."

"Right," Carson said, starting off down the hall. He found several switches and turned on lights as he went. He was opening cupboard doors in the kitchen when a sudden, choked cough reached him. Then there was a thud as of something striking the floor. He tensed, and heard Kildare's voice ring through the house.

"What's that?" the government man demanded.

Carson ran forward toward the front hall and suddenly he was forced to swerve in an effort to keep from stepping on something—something that was crumpled in a heap on the floor. It was Tompkins, the butler!

ANOTHER SUDDEN cry rang through the house, followed by a crash of a window off the living room. Carson ran headlong toward the library door, and at that moment, Kildare charged out automatic in hand. The government man swerved, leaped across the hall into the living room.

A dim light glowed in there, and in its reflection they could see a whole section of one of the front windows smashed to bits, as though a human body had hurled through it. Shouts came from the detectives in other parts of the house, demanding to know what was up.

Then Carson saw Kildare point to a pedestal such as might be used to support a large vase. He stooped beneath the shattered window where the floor was strewn with pieces of a large vase or urn. He picked up the bottom, that was left intact, and placed it on the pedestal.

"Mighty clever trick," Kildare commented. "See that window? It looks as though someone had jumped right through it."

"Yes," Carson nodded, "but what's the idea of the broken vase beneath it?"

Kildare outlined some of the broken sash of the window.

"You see," he said, "there are certain things that make me positive that no one did get through that window. See how the sash is still more or less unbroken? An average human being couldn't get through that opening."

Rod Carson could see that, now that Kildare had called his attention to it. At first, it had looked to him as though the pieces of sash were loose and had flopped back into place, but now he could tell that they were still firm and unbroken.

"The vase," Kildare explained, "was thrown through the window to draw our attention. It was a heavy affair, and was calculated to make a hole in the window as large as a person would make if he leaped through it. Now we'll go back and find out whose trick that was."

"It couldn't have been the butler," Carson said. "He's lying in a heap on the hall floor."

"Yes," Kildare said, "and it couldn't be Justin Brock because he's in the library—dead."

Val Kildare was quite calm, in striking contrast to Carson's excited state.

"Great Scott!" he exploded. "You mean Brock was killed when you were right there beside him in the library?"

Kildare nodded.

"And I think I can explain it all, with possibly one exception," he said. "Come on. We'll see what we find out here."

Kildare was leading the way to the door from the great living room into the hall. They found the detectives clustered around the form of the butler.

"For the love of Mike," they heard one exclaim, "here's another one of those black lilies. The butler's as dead as a doornail!"

Carson leaped across the hall to where two of the detectives were bending over the butler. One looked up and shook his head.

"He's dead, all right," he said.

But Carson was staring at the black blossom of death.

"I don't get it," he cried. "Not more than a minute ago I saw the butler lying here, and the black lotus wasn't on him then. And now—"

"Holy Mackerel!" a detective in the library yelled. "Look here! Kildare! Come here!"

The government man turned wearily toward the nearest library door.

The gray-haired, portly figure of Justin Brock was slumped over sidewise in his chair. One arm hung limply to the floor; the other was in his lap, and in that hand was another black lotus blossom.

"You mean to say," one of the detectives demanded of Kildare, "that you were sitting right here next to Justin Brock when he was killed, and you didn't stop it?"

Kildare nodded.

"That seems to be correct," he admitted.

The detective snorted in disgust.

"And you claim to be a big shot in detecting crime," he said derisively.

"I don't recall making any claim to that effect," Kildare retorted icily, "but I would be very grateful to you if you would explain this whole situation. I imagine it would be quite easy for you."

"Find that guy in the bathrobe and slippers that they call Schuyler," the detective snapped, "and I'll soon have an explanation knocked out of him."

"You are quite sure it was Schuyler?" Kildare asked.

The other flared. "Who else could it be?" he demanded. "There hasn't been anybody else in the house, except you and your friend and the three men that are dead, and Schuyler. He's the only one that we haven't accounted for yet."

Carson saw Kildare's face light up ever so slightly for a moment. The government man took a step sidewise to the left, peered calmly about the library. Carson watched him closely; he could tell by Kildare's expression that something was up.

"Yes," Kildare said to the cocky detective, "but I am inclined to think you wouldn't be any nearer to a solution, if you found Schuyler, than you are now."

"No?" the detective almost shouted, "Well, if you're so clever, you find him and I'll get an explanation out of him."

Kildare shrugged and the slightest trace of a smile played across his thin lips.

"All right," he said calmly, "I'll take you up on that. Try looking behind the davenport here on my left."

"Huh?" the detective exploded.

Then there was a sudden rush, and Carson and the two detectives leaped forward, staring behind the davenport. The light was dim back there, but Carson could see all too plainly.

He heard one of the detectives explode, "For the love of heaven! It's Schuyler! He's dead and he's got a black lily in his hand!"

CHAPTER 8
THE MASS MURDERS

CARSON STARED down at the figure behind the davenport. It was Schuyler all right, still clad in his pajamas and bathrobe. He was lying on the floor, face up. One arm was beside him and the other was across his middle. The hand clutched a black lotus flower.

Carson turned in astonishment and stared at Kildare, but the government man wasn't looking at him. His half-narrowed gray eyes were upon the detective who had challenged him and he was smiling.

"As I recall," he said calmly, "you were going to give me a complete explanation of the whole affair when you found Schuyler."

The detective's face turned red and then purple.

"How did I know he was dead?" he demanded.

"You see," Kildare explained, "you weren't standing in the right spot to see that. But let's lift him up on the davenport. I think we ought to examine his body. We've got to start a complete examination of all the deceased before the coroner gets here, or we won't be able to find out what killed them."

"Do you want me to call the coroner?" the cocky detective asked, his voice taking on a new note of respect for the government man.

"You may as well," Kildare said. "I don't think there are any more to be killed in this house."

As that detective left, two more came in from the hall and bent over the back of the davenport.

"Did you say you wanted him lifted over onto the davenport?" one of them asked.

Kildare nodded but he said nothing, and for some reason that Carson couldn't fathom, he held his fingers to his lips. He made a motion for all the men to stay where they were and not move.

In a loud voice, he said, "Just a minute until I get things ready for the body, then we'll put him on the davenport."

As Carson followed Kildare with his eyes, he saw the government man make a circuit of the library. He was searching the walls, the tables, and the mantel over the fireplace, but apparently he didn't find what he sought. Suddenly, he stopped in front of one of the detectives. The plain clothes man stared at him and frowned.

"Hey, what—" he started to sputter.

But Kildare's hand flew to his lips and covered his mouth. Then, to Carson's amazement, Kildare took hold of the detective's necktie with one hand and with the other he drew a stick pin from it.

"I won't need this for long," he said. "Now I think we are ready. He stepped quickly around to the back of the davenport. "Carson," he said, "you pick up his feet and one of you detectives take him by the shoulders and lift him up. I'll handle his middle. Come on now, easy."

They waited for the signal. "Now," Kildare grunted, "Up over the back of the davenport. That's it."

They lifted him over the back, and prepared to lower him to the cushions. Then Carson saw Kildare's right hand, which held the barbed stick pin, move with lightning speed toward the man's rear. He saw it strike home.

At the same time, Kildare yelled, "Drop him!"

There was a loud cry of pain as the limp body of Schuyler suddenly came to life. His eyes opened and bulged. His mouth was open and he was crying out with pain, but the climax of that cry came when in landing on the sofa, the stick pin was driven in up to the ornamented top.

Schuyler leaped to his feet as though shot upright by a steel spring.

Kildare confronted the alleged friend of Justin Brock.

"Now," he said, "tell us who you are and for whom you're working. Why did Wu Fang send you here, Schuyler?"

Schuyler calmly handed Kildare the stick pin.

"This," he said, "I would like to keep, but of course that would not be permitted where I'm going, so I'll return it."

Without taking his eyes off Schuyler, Kildare took the stick pin and handed it back to the detective from whom he had borrowed it. Schuyler sat back and relaxed.

"I feel a lot more comfortable with that stick pin out," he said. "Let's see, you were asking me some questions about Wu Fang. I'm afraid I can't help you there. I know there is such a person in the Chang Li but I didn't take my orders from him."

"Do you admit," one of the detectives flared, "that you were killing for the Chang Li?"

"Your powers of perception," Schuyler said, "are remarkable,

Inspector. Perhaps you might tell me how all of this was worked out."

"I can tell you," Kildare snapped, "but it won't be necessary at the present time. What I'm going to get from you is the name or names of the members of the Chang Li who gave you these orders. If you name five members of the Chang Li, I'll believe you."

Schuyler shook his head.

"That would hardly be fair," he said. "After all, I have some scruples as to what is right and wrong, and I'll never go back on the Chang Li after the good money they've paid me for the black lotus murders. My only regret is that I can't go on making that money. I suppose now you're going to take me to jail."

Kildare nodded.

"I presume that you won't permit me to get dressed?" Schuyler asked.

"Hardly," Kildare admitted.

"What I want to know," one of the detectives snarled, "is how you came to be in this house in the first place. I understood you were a friend of Justin Brock."

Schuyler smiled.

"That was an idea of my own," he admitted. "You see, I came up here last night. I had a perfectly good detective's badge with me and I told Brock that a detective bureau had sent me here, because we had heard of a plot to kill him and his son. I warned him that no one must know who I was and suggested that he introduce me as a friend of his. The butler, however, was admitted to the secret at the request of Mr. Brock. That's why I had to get him too."

"Do I understand that you were sent here to kill Mr. Brock and his son for the Chang Li, so that they might be avenged for that article in his magazine?"

Schuyler nodded.

"THAT IS correct," he said, "and of course I have explained why I killed the butler. This is merely the beginning of a series of vengeance killings by the Chang Li. You will hear of plenty of deaths before morning, and no matter what you do to me, nothing can stop them."

Carson saw Kildare's muscles tense. His own nerves were on the verge of snapping. The government man's hand shot out to the front of the big fellow's clothing. Schuyler jerked back with a quick move. His right hand came up as though to ward off a blow from Kildare, but it didn't stop at his chest.

"Stop that!" Kildare cried.

Carson sensed what was going on and leaped forward, striking with all his might. His fist caught Schuyler's head between the eyes and snapped it back, but the big man's hand came away from his mouth empty. His eyes glazed, but Carson knew it wasn't from the blow. Schuyler slumped to the davenport.

Kildare's left hand locked around the man's jaw, and tried to pry his mouth open. The body, however, was suddenly growing rigid, and he toppled over on the davenport.

Kildare gave up his efforts and stepped back. He slipped his hand over Schuyler's heart, felt the pulse, then shook his head.

"Well, I guess that finishes him," he concluded. "Now we'll really begin to go into detail."

He began a rapid search of the pockets of both the bathrobe and pajamas, but except for a handkerchief, he found nothing.

Carson could smell an odor that had been quite strong, as he recalled, since he had first entered the house. It was like the smell of a flower and had a slightly musty tang.

"That odor," Kildare said, sniffing the air, "gave me the real suspicion that Schuyler, or whatever his real name was, had something to do with the death of young Roger Brock. I smelled that odor when I was near him in the hall. It's the odor of the black lotus, and I'm positive now that he had three black lotus blossoms under his bathrobe at the time. You can still smell them on his clothing."

"I can't see yet," Carson admitted, "how he committed these murders. We don't even know what killed the two Brocks and the butler."

"No, that's right," Kildare admitted, staring down at the white face of Schuyler on the davenport. His brow furrowed; he was deep in thought.

Without a word, he walked calmly around the head of the davenport and stood looking behind it for almost a minute. He slid in behind the back and crouched down. Carson heard him say, "H'm." Then he saw the government man reach in under the davenport and pick something off the floor. He came up with two objects in his hand. One was a little metal container, almost like a half-sized cigarette case. The other was a small tube. It looked not unlike an ordinary straw that one uses at a soda fountain, except that it was twice as long and a bit heavier. Kildare held it up.

"Do you know what this is?" he asked.

Instantly, Carson recognized it.

"It's called a sarbacane," he said. "It's a very small one at that, but I'll gamble it's mighty accurate if someone knows how to use it."

"A sarbacane?" one of the detectives growled. "I never heard of such a thing."

"In plain language," Kildare explained, "it's a blow gun. Some of them are ten times as large as this. I have heard of them being ten or twelve feet long, and then again, they make them even smaller than this one. This, you see, is very finely made of split bamboo. These blow guns are used by the South American Indians and the yaks of Borneo."

The detectives and Carson gathered around Kildare and stared into the box. There, set in separate stalls made of coarsely-carded jute, were tiny pellets no more than a sixteenth of an inch in diameter and perhaps a quarter of an inch long.

Kildare touched one with the end of the blow pipe. It was soft and gelatinous. He held the box up to his nostrils and sniffed.

"That's a new one on me," he admitted. "But then, these orientals can concoct deadly poisons much faster than we."

"But how the deuce does a thing like that work?" one of the detectives blurted out. "I thought you had to get poison inside of you."

"This could be worked very simply," Kildare explained. He

moved over toward the body of the publisher, Justin Brock. Gently, he raised the body to a sitting posture until the head lolled against the back of the chair. Even now the lips were parted.

"I WAS asking Mr. Brock to tell me what he had feared before we came," Kildare explained. "Of course, that's apparent now from what this murderer"—he jerked his head toward Schuyler's body—"told us. Brock was just in the act of telling me and had just opened his mouth to speak when we heard the sound of the butler choking and falling to the floor."

Kildare picked up a light and held it over in front of Brock's face. Carefully, he moved the jaw down so that the mouth was open wide, and stared inside.

"Look," he said. He backed away and pointed with the blow pipe to an almost infinitesimal gelatinous speck near the tip of the tongue. Carson saw it immediately.

"Why, that's what's left of one of these pellets," he said.

"Yes," Kildare nodded. "Evidently, it takes only a very small portion of whatever these pellets contain, to kill."

"Say, listen, don't try to kid me," one of the detectives cut in. "Do you mean to tell me that somebody could stand off with a blow pipe and shoot one of those things right into Brock's mouth?"

"Expert users of the blow pipe," Kildare reminded him, "can aim them as accurately as an expert rifleman. Only, of course, they haven't quite the range. And here's something else that you will probably recall, Carson." Kildare turned to the young explorer.

"Remember, young Roger Brock had his mouth open when he was killed. He had just said 'Hello,' and he was going to say 'Schuyler,' or something like that, when the pellet hit him. That apparently came from close range. Let's have a look."

They went out into the hall. Kildare turned young Brock's body over and turned his flash on it. He nodded. Carson could see the same thing—a tiny bit of gelatin-like formation still lying on the tip of his tongue.

"Let's see how the butler came out," Kildare suggested.

He led the way down to the rear of the hall to where Tompkins' body lay, but here was something different. The butler's mouth wasn't open, but his tongue protruded between his lips as though he had been wetting them. He had died in the act. Kildare shook his head.

"That's about the most deadly thing I ever saw in my life," he said. "Evidently, you only have to touch this poison to a person's lips. If my guess is correct, the poisonous substance, if it misses the mouth, make the victim want to lick his lips, and the minute his tongue touches the poison, he's done. You see, the tongue is like a sponge. There are quite a few poisons that will kill if even a small portion is placed on the tongue, because the absorption into the system is very rapid."

But Carson was still puzzled, and he received a grateful look from two of the detectives when he said, "I'd like to know how all this killing was managed, Kildare. I think you have it all figured out?"

"Oh, yes," Kildare nodded. "I nearly forgot."

He jerked his head toward the body of the young man as he

continued, "Roger Brock, apparently, was partially under the influence of liquor, and his reactions weren't quick enough when he saw Schuyler raise the pipe to his lips. What stumped me for a while was the fact that I was sitting in the library talking to Mr. Brock, and when we heard the butler cry out, I could see part of Schuyler's bathrobe as he stood near the door. But I couldn't see his face and took for granted that he couldn't do anything at that distance. Then, immediately after I heard the butler fall, I turned my attention to that disturbance. I forgot Justin Brock, who was sitting next to me for the moment, and that was Schuyler's chance to poke his blow pipe past one side of the drapes at the edge of the doorway and drive a pellet between Brock's lips.

"When I heard him gasp, I turned, but Schuyler must have run into the living room on the other side of the hall, for I couldn't see him. He picked up the big vase that stood on the pedestal and hurled it through the window to draw our attention to the living room. When we ran in and were staring at the broken window in the front, Schuyler was hiding behind a chair or some other large piece of furniture. Then, slipping out into the hall behind us, he placed a lotus flower in the butler's hand as a sweet token of affection from the Chang Li. Then he entered the library through the corner door and left a flower in Justin Brock's hand.

"Things were coming pretty fast then, and he knew he wouldn't have time to get out, so he dropped down on his back behind the davenport, took the last black lotus from under his bathrobe and placed that in his own hand.

"Of course, he hid the blow pipe and the pellets under the davenport so there wouldn't be any evidence on his body, if he were discovered to be alive."

Kildare shrugged.

"That seems to be about all there is—"

He stopped short as an insistent pounding on the front door came to them. Carson leaped to open it and swung it wide. Three men—coroner's assistants—entered. The deputy coroner in charge looked questioningly at the body of Tompkins and Roger Brock. Carson saw his eyes open wide and then narrow as they spotted the two black lotus blossoms.

"Say what is this, a game?" he demanded. "These two stiffs make eleven we have had to take care of this morning. And everyone of them has been decorated up with a black lily."

CHAPTER 9
THE HAIRLESS VISITOR

JERRY HAZARD had taken Mohra, escorted by a heavy police squad, to an apartment next to his own.

"I'm afraid, darling," he said as he led her into the living room of the apartment, "that you won't have much privacy for a while." He turned quickly to the officer standing at the open door and nodded significantly. The big, red-faced Irish patrolman grinned and nodded back.

"Five minutes," he said.

Hazard turned to Mohra. He seized her suddenly in his arms

and held her tight. For nearly a minute neither spoke, then Mohra pushed him away a little, reluctantly.

"I won't mind being under heavy guard, Jerry," she said. "I won't mind anything, so long as you are with me."

"Listen, darling," Hazard pleaded, "We're together now, you and I. Let's be married now, at once. Why must we wait any longer?"

Mohra shook her head.

"You know, Jerry," she said, "there's nothing I would like better but we can't—not yet. Not until it's definitely proven that Wu Fang is dead. I have told you before, that so long as Wu Fang is alive, it wouldn't be fair to either of us."

Hazard opened his mouth to argue further but Mohra raised her hand and placed two cool, soft fingers on his lips. Then she took his face in her hands and kissed him again.

Far too soon, a knock sounded on the door, and a rich Irish voice said, "Sure, and your five minutes were past long ago, and we were put in charge of the young lady to see that she's kept safe. We'll be catching the devil himself from the captain if anything happens to her this time." Hazard and Mohra parted reluctantly.

"Come on in," Hazard said. He led an inspection of the apartment.

The living room had two windows opening on a court There were two windows in the bedroom, but they opened on a corner of the building.

It was hot and close in the bedroom. He threw open one of the windows and started to look out to make sure the wall, for eight stories below, was unscalable. As he leaned forward with his hands on the window sill, a voice came to him from the black void of the court below.

"Mr. Hazard."

That was all. For a split second, Jerry Hazard hesitated at the window sill and stared out, trying to locate the direction from which the sound had come. Suddenly something swished past his face. He ducked back and his hand flew to the window and closed it. His heart was pounding like mad. That had been a close shave!

He turned to the two officers who were in the bedroom with him and explained, "Something just swished past my face. I think it was a poison dart. It seemed to come up from the court."

He turned and studied the line of flight that the missile must have taken in coming through the window and past his head.

"A long range shot," he said. "That's why they weren't very accurate. I want to try and find out what it is."

He reached up and pulled the shade of the window down.

"We'll leave it like that for a few minutes," he said.

He stepped in front of the window again, struck another line with his hand, pointed to the other side of the room.

"There," he said to the officer who was standing near the spot, his hand indicated. "Let's have a look at that drape beside you."

He crossed the floor and they inspected the drape minutely, but they could find nothing that might have flashed past Hazard's face.

"Look here," the other officer said. He pointed to a tiny spot on the wall, rubbed it with his fingers. "Looks like a little daub of jelly," he observed.

The cop raised his fingers toward his lips but Hazard leaped forward and knocked his arm down.

"Hey, what's the idea?" the cop demanded.

"You don't want to die, do you?" Hazard asked curtly.

"Certainly not," the cop retorted.

Hazard and Mohra stared horror-stricken at the strange figure.

"You were going to taste that stuff, weren't you?" Hazard asked.

"Well, that little speck couldn't have hurt me."

"How do you know?" Hazard demanded. "I have seen simpler things than that, with which Wu Fang killed people."

"Yen," said the cop, "but how did Wu Fang know we were here?"

"Don't ask me to explain the impossible," Hazard snapped.

The sergeant entered the bedroom and Hazard showed him what had happened.

"I'll tell you what I want you to do," he said. "Send two men back to headquarters to get a couple of search lights. I want them played constantly on the windows of this apartment, particularly those of the bedroom, until daylight."

"Say," the sergeant nodded. "That's a good idea. I'll take care of it at once." Hazard heard him dispatching two of the officers to carry out his orders.

Mohra was white-faced and trembling as she met Hazard in the living room.

"What happened in there?" she asked.

Hazard tried to laugh it off, but he knew his laughter didn't sound sincere.

"Don't worry, Mohra," he said. "Everything is going to be all right. I'm going to stay with you until morning. It will soon be daylight and you aren't apt to have much trouble then. Are you sleepy?"

"No," Mohra said, shaking her head, "but I'll try to turn in and get some sleep, if you think I should."

"No," Hazard said quickly. "You aren't going to sleep in that bedroom. Lie here on the davenport and get what rest and sleep you can. The police and I are going to be close to you, and I don't think we'll have much trouble after they get the search lights rigged up."

But an hour went by, and still no search light beams shot up at the windows of the apartment. Then there came an ear-splitting yell from below.

The sergeant and his men rushed across the room, but Hazard uttered a warning cry, "Don't open those windows!"

AS HE spoke, he was sitting on the edge of the davenport where Mohra was lying, and the automatic that Kildare had returned to him was in his hand. One of the cops didn't seem to hear him, for he placed his hands on the sash as though he were going to raise the window and look out. A sharp command from Jerry Hazard checked him.

The sergeant turned, and his face was a little white as he said, "Something has happened to the two men whom I sent to fix up those search lights."

"Then send two more to find out what it is," Hazard snapped. "But don't open the window. You can't see anything from here anyway."

The sergeant gave hasty orders and two more men were dispatched.

"Shoot first and ask questions later," the sergeant ordered.

The two cops left, and fifteen minutes passed uneventfully. Then they heard a commotion among the officers who were guarding the door of the apartment. Somebody was talking excitedly, but they couldn't catch the words. Suddenly the door burst open and one of the last two officers to leave came staggering into the room.

"Sergeant!" he gasped. "For the love of heaven, something awful has happened. We found Mulligan and Kablosky. They're both dead and they've each got a black lily in their hand. O'Flynn and I tried to get the search lights working, when I saw a movement over in the back of the alley, about ten or fifteen feet away.

"The next thing I knew, O'Flynn fell over on his face. Then I spotted something in the beam of the flash light—the most devilish thing I have ever seen in my life, sergeant. It looked like a monkey, but it didn't have any hair. The thing started right up the side of the building and disappeared before I could get a shot at him."

Mohra was sitting up now, wild-eyed and pale. She was clinging to Hazard, and the newspaper man nodded toward the frightened officer.

"Better get him out of here, Sergeant," he suggested. "I'll call for more men."

The sergeant nodded and turned the frightened policeman over to another officer.

"Better take him back to headquarters." Then he turned to Hazard. "You'd better let me call up for reinforcements," he said. "They might not believe you."

The police sergeant picked up the phone, jiggled the receiver, and shouted into the mouthpiece. Then he shook his head.

"Phone's dead," he said with a sort of sickly expression on his face. He slammed up the receiver and tore out into the hall.

"Hey, you," he shouted to the nerve-shattered officer and the one who was taking him back to the station, "Tell the captain we can use about twenty-five more men here. And you'd better tell them to send the coroner over to look after O'Flynn and Mulligan and Kablosky."

Then the sergeant came back and slammed the door.

"What do we do now?" he asked. It was plain that he was completely baffled.

Hazard was trying hard to think of a plan.

"It's only an unnecessary risk to go out there and try to fix up the search lights," he said. "The best thing I can suggest is to turn out the lights in the apartment, put up the shades and leave the windows closed. I'm going to sit here on the davenport with Mohra. I've got a gun, and if anything shows on the outside of these windows, I'm going to blast away. Keep two officers at the door to the hall and one a little way down the corridor as a reserve. You can take your other man and go into the bedroom. Each of you stand by a window with your guns cocked, and if anything appears on the window ledge, shoot to kill. You'll be able to see them in the reflection of the street lights, but they won't be able to see you—I hope."

Minutes dragged on into an hour. Finally, the sergeant's voice came from the bedroom.

"Ought to be hearing from those re-enforcements I asked for," he said. "That is, if my two men ever reached headquarters."

But the time dragged on. Another hour passed, and another.

Mohra had been sitting very close to Jerry all this time. At last she had fallen asleep, and Hazard lowered her gently to the davenport.

Twice Jerry Hazard reached for the phone and picked it up, but each time the line was dead. Suddenly, he was sitting up more tensely, his hand grasping the butt of his automatic.

Something had moved outside that window—something that he could see outlined plainly in the light. At first he thought it was a little beast shaped like a rat. He saw it just above the lower edge of the window sash. It was coming up over the outside sill, and he remembered now that the sill wasn't more than six inches wide. Suddenly he remembered something else!

That window over there wasn't locked. He remembered that he had meant to lock it before the lights went off and had forgotten it. He saw that it might be possible to pry the lower sash up an inch or so without attracting the attention of anyone inside. Once that sash was open, anything might happen. A blow-pipe stuck in the opening could do the trick very nicely.

He leaned forward, finger pressed against the trigger. Again he saw something move just above the bottom sash. Two small hands like those of a child were grasping the sill.

Now something else rose above the lower edge of the sash—something round, like the top of an ostrich egg. But Hazard knew that it was a head, gaunt and hairless. Next, scrawny shoulders appeared, and then he could see the arms of the being as it held itself to the outside sill and tried to peer into the room.

A short leg came up and was perched there for an instant.

One of the hands held a small tube—a blow pipe! The other foot came up, and the ghastly, naked figure of a being that seemed half monkey, half man, balanced outside the window.

Hazard, for a moment, was frozen in horror. The hands of the beast were on the sash. There came the crash of breaking glass.

Only one set of muscles in Hazard's horror-stricken body moved. Those controlled his trigger finger.

Blam! Blam! Blam!

There was another shatter of glass, and he heard Mohra cry out as she awoke behind him. The figure at the window swung out into space and then vanished, emitting a hideous scream.

The sergeant and the other police officer came running out from the bedroom. Mohra was clinging to Hazard, asking him if he was all right. He explained to the sergeant what had happened.

And Hazard finished, "I don't blame your officer for getting the jitters after he saw that beastly thing. It's the most ghastly creature I ever saw. I hope I killed it."

CHAPTER 10
GARDEN OF THE
BLACK LOTUS

THERE WAS no more sleep for Mohra the rest of that night. She sat close beside Hazard until dawn came, but there was no more evidence of the hairless marauder.

Mohra prepared breakfast in the little kitchenette for her

protectors, and they had just finished eating when Kildare and Carson came in. Hazard frowned as he stared at the drawn, white face of the government man.

"For heaven's sake, Kildare," he exploded, "I never saw you look like that. Something pretty bad must have happened."

"Yes," Kildare admitted, "it is pretty bad. We had a real epidemic of murders before daylight this morning."

He told them briefly of what happened at the Brock mansion.

"Then the coroner arrived," he finished, "and told us of nine other black lotus murders. Since then we've heard of five more, and all the reports aren't in yet."

Mohra uttered a little choked cry.

"Oh," she gasped, "this is terrible! And you mean that they were all killed by Wu Fang?"

Kildare shook his head.

"I don't know," he said, "I'm pretty well stumped, but I'm quite sure that Wu Fang is responsible."

"It was certainly Wu Fang's agents, using his methods, that tried to get up here this morning before daylight," Hazard said. He and the police sergeant told Kildare what had happened at the apartment.

Kildare nodded to the sergeant. "I think you can safely take your men off duty now. Go to headquarters and report what's happened. Have the telephone wire repaired, and send a fresh guard of about eight officers and another sergeant to watch Mohra."

The police were preparing to leave when Kildare turned to Hazard and said, "I think you will want to go with me this morning. I'm going to make a little call on a Chinaman. He's a member of the Chang Li."

"You mean Wu Fang?" Hazard asked quickly.

"No," Kildare said, "but this Chinaman may be able to tell us what is going on."

"But, why all these killings?" Hazard demanded. "Are they people who have offended the Chang Li or Wu Fang?"

"No," Kildare answered. "That's the queer part of it. Brock and his son were obviously killed because they published that article in the Weekly Post, and the butler died because he knew too much. But let's go over some other people who were murdered. There are, for instance, men like David Gandel."

Hazard leaned forward as he asked quickly, "You mean the president of the B. and L. railroad, who has been in the newspapers so much recently?"

Kildare nodded.

"And that's another funny thing," he said. "Except for the five cops that were killed outside this apartment house, and Brock's butler, every victim has been quite prominent in the newspapers lately. There's George Pellett, the famous aviator, and Hugh R. Morgan, the banker. The rest run in that same line, although I can't possibly figure what they have to do with the case in any way."

"And you mean," Hazard demanded, "that in every case the parties were found dead with a black lotus in their hands?"

"That's what the coroner told us," Carson said.

"And yet you say you don't blame Wu Fang for that," Mohra cried.

Kildare turned to her and smiled.

"I didn't exactly say that, Mohra," he said. "I admit that I am pretty well baffled, and I can't figure just who is to blame."

"All the deaths were from the same cause?" Hazard asked.

"Yes," Kildare nodded. "All from those little gelatin pellets that struck the victims either in the mouth or on their lips."

Kildare stepped over to one of the big chairs in the living room, slumped down in it, and lighted one of his long, slim cigars. He puffed thoughtfully for a few moments and then laid it aside.

"I'm going to catch a few winks of sleep until the new detachment of police arrives," he said. "I think we'll be perfectly safe here in the daylight."

Hazard shook his head.

"I'm dead for sleep," he confessed, "but I couldn't close my eyes on a bet."

Kildare didn't answer; he was suddenly dead to the world, breathing easily and regularly. Carson, Hazard, and Mohra talked matters over, trying to figure out a solution, but to no avail.

The officers came to guard Mohra, and as though their arrival was an alarm, Kildare snapped out of it. He was instantly wide awake and giving orders.

"Now, remember," he told the new sergeant. "You are on duty in the daytime. I don't think you're going to have any trouble, but under no circumstances must you leave the young lady alone."

He turned to Mohra. "You must not leave this apartment

today," he said. "Provisions will be brought up and you can have meals sent up, too, if you wish."

An express subway train took Kildare, Carson and Hazard down to the edge of Chinatown.

"I have been to see this gentleman once before," Kildare told Carson and Hazard. "I don't believe you have ever met him, Jerry, and I am sure you haven't met him, Carson. Face to face, I mean. But I want you to listen to him when he speaks. I think you will recognize his voice. His name is Wong Chu."

On the outside, Wong Chu's house was dull and drab-looking, much like the other dirty two and three story buildings that line the narrow twisting streets of Chinatown. But the eyes of Hazard and Kildare opened wide as they noted the sudden change in the interior.

A GIANT Chinese, a servant of Wong Chu, ushered them into a great reception hall. Priceless hangings, rare pieces of statuary and incredibly beautiful rugs were blended into a general effect of tasteful magnificence. The great Chinese servant bowed as he admitted them.

Kildare gave him his name, told him he wished to see Wong Chu. The huge Chinaman bowed and closed the heavy door. Another menial, clad in oriental garb, came noiselessly from a side room. The first servant spoke to the second in Chinese, and the latter vanished.

The one who had admitted them stood with his back to the door, arms folded across his massive chest. From somewhere off in the house a gong sounded. There were three muffled, deep-throated bongs, and as though that were a signal, the great servant bowed again.

"You will follow, honorable sirs," he said. He turned abruptly and led the way through a wide door, to the rear of the hall. Just inside that entrance he bowed again.

Now the servant stepped aside and the three men advanced through the door.

Hazard felt his feet sink deep into an enormous, blue Chinese rug. In a carved ebony chair, sat a Chinaman of very slight build. He was a wiry little fellow with a pleasant face. He was getting up, now, and it was easy to see that he was a man of importance, for he had that bearing about him. He smiled and walked toward Kildare, holding out his hand.

"I am happy to have you call upon me again," he said to the government man.

"We may as well come to cases, Wong Chu," Kildare smiled. "You know why I am here."

Wong Chu hesitated.

"Perhaps you have come to sip a cup of tea," he suggested. "Should I know the answer, honorable Mr. Kildare?"

"I think," Kildare said, "after what happened last night and this morning, you should know, Wong Chu."

"You are accusing me, Mr. Kildare?"

"No," the government man said. "Nothing of the kind." He turned suddenly to Carson and asked, "Do you recognize the voice?"

"Yes," Carson nodded. "I'd know it anywhere, and if I had

had my way, he would at least have a terrible headache this morning."

The wiry little Chinaman continued to smile. Nothing seemed to anger him. He was apparently in perfect control of his emotions.

"This is one of the leaders of the parade last night," Carson explained to Hazard.

"Yes, I remember," Hazard nodded, "and I recognize his voice, too. It was this man Wong Chu, with the big head disguising his face, who quieted the members of the Chang Li after I broke up the parade and found Mohra in the casket."

And now, strangely enough, Wong Chu nodded in agreement.

"That is correct," he said. "I was the one. Mr. Kildare knows already that I am one of the high commanders of the Chang Li."

"You are *the* high commander," Carson corrected. "We saw you running the whole show in the temple."

"I believe, Mr. Carson," Wong Chu said, "that you said something about a headache. May I assure you that I have a headache this morning, though through no fault of yours. As you Americans use the word, I understand that it means a lot of trouble, does it not?"

"That's the way I understand it," Kildare assured him with a smile.

"Then I have, indeed, a headache this morning," Wong Chu continued.

"Just what do you mean?" Kildare asked.

"Let us go into the garden," Wong Chu suggested. "Perhaps it will be more pleasant there."

Jerry Hazard couldn't help feeling that the Chinaman had some particular reason for getting them into the garden, and the moment he entered it, he was positive. Except for the high brick walls of the windowless buildings that surrounded it on three sides, it might have been a little spot of the most beautiful section of the earth.

EVERYTHING IN it was oriental. There was a pagoda on the right, a small affair with seats for two. In front of it was a shallow little pool, and this drew the instant attention of the three guests. Hazard stared in amazement at the foliage that grew in the shallow water. There were great, green leaves on stiff stems, and one blossom—a blossom that he had seen before. It was a luxuriant black lotus.

He heard Carson exclaim, "Great Scott! A death flower!"

But Wong Chu took no notice of his remark. He motioned to a little table with four chairs about it, at the left side of the pool.

"The tea will be here in a minute," he said. "Will you sit down, honorable gentlemen?"

Wong Chu was the last to take his place at the little table. The servant reentered with a black wood tray and placed little cups of tea before them. He set a plate of Chinese cakes in the middle of the table and glided noiselessly away.

Leisurely, their host finished his tea, passed cigarettes, and sat back in his chair. He smiled and waited a moment, then his quick eyes flashed to Carson's face.

"Your mention of a headache, Mr. Carson," he said, "reminded me of my garden."

Wong Chu's small hand moved in a graceful gesture toward the pool and the lone black blossom.

"The black lotus, Mr. Carson, is not a death flower," he explained. "It has never been considered as such by the Chang Li. It is a sacred flower, yes, but the black lotus has nothing to do with death. Perhaps I may explain a little more clearly when I tell you that the Chang Li was organized over a thousand years ago for a special purpose. That purpose is one of our secrets, but it is quite generally known that the original organizer of the Chang Li was the first man to develop the black lotus flower. No one except a member of the Chang Li was ever permitted to know the secret of the cultivation of this rare plant.

"The black lotus has been stolen by our enemies many times, but without the secret of cultivation, and the flower and the plant degenerated so that future flowers were not a pure black but rather a dull blue. So, as I say, no one in the world who is not a member of the Chang Li, with one exception, can raise the black lotus. And I repeat, it is not a death flower; rather, it is our badge of hope and faith."

Hazard saw Carson open his mouth to speak, but Kildare shut him off with another warning glance. But Wong Chu had seen Carson's lips part and his smile broadened.

"I know, of course, what you were going to say, Mr. Carson," he said. "You were about to ask why it is, then, that so many deaths occurred last night and this morning, and in each case this flower of the black lotus was found upon the deceased. I am coming to that presently."

He swept his hand again toward the pool and the black lotus leaves with the single blossom.

"That, then, is what you call my headache," he said. "You think perhaps I have been a poor member of the Chang Li—that I have not been a good horticulturist—that I have not been able to raise but one black lotus? But that is not so. Last night when I left my home and my beloved garden to go to the parade, I counted the blossoms in the pool. There were fifty seven. I was very proud, honorable sirs, of my flowers. The greatest display of black lotus in the whole world was right here in my own little garden. But when I returned from the temple before sunrise this morning, I found only one blossom left. All of the others had been stolen."

Hazard saw Kildare suddenly jerk upright in his chair.

"Stolen?" the government man exclaimed.

CHAPTER 11
SATAN'S SIGNATURE

THE ATMOSPHERE in the quiet little garden was suddenly tinged with excitement. Kildare seldom was aroused to that state where he snapped out a question as he did now, and on top of that question came another.

"There's a lot you haven't told us yet, Wong Chu," he said. Wong Chu nodded.

"Before I finish, I will explain all of it to you," he said.

"You mentioned the fact that, with one exception, no one knows how to cultivate the black lotus except members of the Chang Li," Kildare said. "What did you mean by that?"

Wong Chu turned in his chair so that he faced Kildare directly.

"Permit me, honorable Mr. Kildare, to go back a few hours," he said "I think you will realize that what I am saying is true and will check with what you already know. I will take you back, if you please, to the moment when you entered the temple of the Chang Li. I believe you heard much excited talk, as though someone were very angry. You recognized the voice of the speaker as that of Wu Fang. That talk of Wu Fang was prompted by something that happened only a few minutes before you entered.

"In our parade it is imperative that we have the effigy of Sun Hu Chek, our enemy of a thousand years past. Wu Fang was appointed head of the committee to arrange the effigy in the coffin, and in that way he was successful in substituting the drugged body of the young lady. Through your efforts, Mr. Hazard, we discovered the mistake.

"A hurried meeting of the governors, of which I am the head, was called. All this took place after the discovery and before the ceremony. It was my privilege to announce the misconduct of Wu Fang, and, as a result, he was voted out of the Chang Li, making him an outcast of the organization.

"When he was talking angrily at the back door, he was hurling threats at me and the other members, particularly the governors. You know what happened after that. After you were ushered out of the temple, we continued with the rites of the sacrifice. That lasted for two or three hours.

"When I came home I found that my garden had been stripped of every black lotus except this one. Several of my friends who are influential in the Chang Li and who also have very fine black lotus gardens, have called to tell me that in each case their gardens have been robbed of every flower but one."

Rod Carson shot out a pertinent question, "How many lotus blossoms does that make in all that have been stolen?"

Wong Chu thought for a moment.

"I am not sure of the exact number," he said, "but I think it comes to a little over two hundred."

"That means, then, that for everyone of those black lotus blossoms that have been stolen a death will occur perhaps today or tonight," Kildare exclaimed.

"Yes, that is correct. I see that you understand what I am trying to explain, honorable Mr. Kildare. I believe that you understand what I am trying to explain, honorable Mr. Kildare. I believe that you realize I am telling the truth."

"I don't doubt it for a moment," Kildare assured him. "I see the picture very clearly, and everything is explained. I am sure Wu Fang is causing these murders for his own satisfaction. He's directing the suspicion against the Chang Li to retaliate for their excommunication of him."

"That is correct," Wong Chu nodded. "I am quite sure I know of one entrance to Wu Fang's hiding place. If you gentlemen wish, I will be only too glad to direct you there, tonight."

"Excellent," Kildare said.

"I take it, then, that we of the Chang Li will no longer be held responsible, that our name is—"

Suddenly Wong Chu ceased talking as a babble of voices came from the front part of the house. They could hear the sound of arguing.

A deep, bellowing voice roared, "Get out of my way, you yellow devil, or I'll drill you with this automatic."

"We want to know where Wong Chu is," another rasped. "Show us the way or we'll string you higher than a kite."

"Be advised that Wong Chu is not in, honorable gentlemen," came the calm reply of the servant. "He has gone away. What do you wish? What shall I tell him?"

"He's here all right," a burly voice growled. "Kildare was seen coming in and he hasn't left the place. As long as he's here, Wong Chu is here."

"Isn't there some way you can get out, Wong Chu?" Kildare hissed. "That's the voice of one of the chief inspectors. Those policemen are in a nasty temper. They think that you're the man behind all these crimes. We're going to need you badly."

Wong Chu shook his head.

"There is no way out," he said. "But wait—perhaps I can—"

He started toward the pagoda, but a deep-throated, bellowing voice stopped him in his tracks.

"Another step, Chink, and you die."

Val Kildare stepped forward in his usual suave manner. "Just a minute, Inspector," he said calmly.

"A MINUTE, nothing," the big, square-jawed detective countered. He had a police revolver in his hand and it was leveled at Wong Chu. "You talked us out of getting this bird and his pals once before. If we had had him and the rest in the jug last night before midnight, there would be fourteen of fifteen more people alive today."

"You'll appear a lot less ridiculous if you don't talk like a child," Kildare said.

"So I'm talking like a child?" the inspector roared. "Well, you'll see when we convict this guy."

"You are making an awful mistake, Inspector," Kildare said.

"Maybe you want to tell us all about it, wise guy," the inspector flared. "Who was behind all the killings?"

Kildare hesitated a moment, then shook his head.

"No, it wouldn't do any good to tell you," he said. "You'd only abuse the information that I gave you. I might better keep it to myself and work on it unhindered."

At that moment, a half dozen plain clothes detectives came crowding through the door into the garden. Hazard saw that their eyes took in, among other things, the lone black lotus growing in the garden.

"This is a cinch," one said decisively.

Then the chief inspector suddenly turned on Kildare.

"And listen," he said, "maybe you're in on this."

"Certainly, I am," Kildare retorted. "I'm as guilty as Wong Chu."

Two of the detectives snapped handcuffs on Wong Chu's wrists.

"There's no use hanging around here any longer," the chief

said. "If you want to argue any more about this, Kildare, you can take it up with the commissioner."

"Thanks for the tip," Kildare nodded. "I may do that."

Twenty minutes later, Kildare was in the commissioner's office, but the police chief was out of town. He made several other calls on high officials of the police department, but none would take the responsibility of releasing Wong Chu.

It was noon when Kildare sent Hazard and Carson to get some sleep. They met again that evening at Mohra's apartment.

"There doesn't seem to be much that I can do," Kildare told them, shaking his head sadly. "I'd start right now after Wu Fang if I knew where to go."

"Won't Wong Chu tell you now?" Carson demanded.

"No," Kildare said. "The whole police force has certainly gotten up on their ear over this thing. They refuse to let me talk to him. I did manage to get him a lawyer but they refused him bail at any price."

Kildare stopped short and spun around.

"The mayor and I used to get along pretty well together," he said thoughtfully. "He has been out of his office twice when I called, but I'm going to try and get in touch with him at his home."

Hazard saw Kildare stride over and pick up the phone, heard him call the mayor's house.

Then he was saying, "Kildare speaking. I want to talk to the mayor. That's right. I can't talk to him? Why? What?—No!—How long ago?—Twenty minutes?—Right!"

Kildare hung up the phone and turned with a peculiar expression on his face.

"The mayor is dead," he announced tersely.

"Dead?" the others cried in unison.

"RIGHT," KILDARE nodded. "Dead. Not only that, but it's another black lotus murder. That was the coroner's assistant on the phone, the same one that was at the Brock mansion early this morning." He turned to Carson as he asked, "You remembered our friend Schuyler who committed the murders there?"

Carson's teeth clenched.

"I'll never forget him," he said grimly.

"Schuyler has vanished. The coroner said he walked right out of the morgue after they got him down there."

"Why, that's impossible," Carson exploded.

Hazard shook his head.

"Not with Wu Fang, it isn't," he countered. "You and Kildare probably thought he took some kind of a poison, but he didn't. It was one of Wu Fang's mysterious chemicals that gives the human body the appearance of death."

Suddenly, Kildare turned to Jerry Hazard. "Jerry, you've got to go down to the syndicate office with me," he said. "It's mighty important."

The telephone bell jangled and Kildare leaped to answer it."

"Yes, this is Kildare," he said. "What is it?" Yes, yes, go on— What?"

Hazard saw him nod his head. An ominous hush fell over the room as they waited.

"Good Lord!" Kildare groaned. "O.K.—thanks."

116

The receiver slammed down on the hook again and the government man spun around.

"That just bears out what I was going to say, Jerry," he said. "Two more murders and it isn't eight o'clock yet."

"Who?" was the chorused question.

"Nelson Davenport, the famous actor and Thomas McCloskey, the president's right hand man here in New York."

"Good Lord!" Hazard breathed. "Why, those two men have occupied the front pages of the newspapers all over the country for the last few months."

"That's exactly what I mean," Kildare nodded emphatically. "We've got to rush over to the syndicate office and make out a complete list of names of the people who have figured prominently in the news lately."

"I don't get it," Hazard said, frowning.

Kildare explained. "He's picking his victims from a list of names of the people who have figured most prominently in the news in the last month or two—the people whose death will cause the most excitement when they're killed. He's going to get the entire population of the United States in an uproar against the Chang Li, and he thinks we're going to help him. What we've got to do is to get down to your syndicate office, Jerry, dig out the names of all the prominent figures in the news and notify those people as rapidly as we can. From there, with the influence of your syndicate behind us, we will spread the news by radio and every other possible means of communication. Come on! Carson and I will go with you."

"I'm sorry, Kildare," Jerry said, "but I've got Mohra at last and I'm going to stay with her, now."

"Jerry," Kildare pleaded. "Listen to me, fellow. Do you realize that you may save hundreds of lives by doing this? We've got to get the warning out, and you're the only one that can go down to your syndicate office and put the thing over. The police don't trust me any longer. They think I've ruined their case already and I can't get any help from them. Mohra will be all right here. The officers will stay with her every minute."

Mohra added her urging to Kildare's.

"Yes," she said, "you've got to go, Jerry. I want you to go. It wouldn't be fair for you to stay here with me when you can save the lives of others. Please go!"

"O. K.," Hazard agreed. "Here."

He handed his automatic to her.

"Keep that and don't let anyone talk you into letting go of it. If anyone threatens you, let him have it. I'll try to be back as soon as I can."

CHAPTER 12
A NIGHT OF TERROR

TELEGRAPH INSTRUMENTS clattered and rattled; typewriters hummed; office boys ran frantically from desk to desk. A dozen special writers were pounding typewriters as fast as their fingers could hit the keys.

Kildare stared about the interior of the great office of the

McNulty Syndicate for which Jerry Hazard was a special cor-respondent. He shook his head slowly.

"Tough spot," he said. "I never saw so much action in a newspaper office in my life."

Jerry Hazard passed through the sacred portals into the private office of the syndicate head himself to tell him what Kildare wanted. One—two minutes passed. Then, suddenly, the door flew open and Hazard motioned to Carson and Kildare. The two strode rapidly into the office.

Hazard introduced them to his chief, a man of apparently slow action, but whom Kildare knew to be a human dynamo.

"I didn't get Jerry's story very straight," the chief said. "Now just what is it that you want?"

Kildare hurriedly explained, "It's a matter of life and death to everyone who has been prominent in the news recently. The first thing we've got to do is to get word to them. Now, here are the plans as I have figured them out. Everyone who is in danger must tie a handkerchief about his nose and mouth; keep under cover behind locked doors; get a gun and use it if anyone should threaten him."

The telephone bell on the desk jangled. The chief picked it up.

"Go on," he said. Into the mouthpiece, he said, "Yeah?"

"We've got to get these orders out," Kildare rushed on, "di-rectly by telephone to these people. Then we've got to send a general warning to everyone over the radio."

In answer to something that had come over the phone, the chief whistled.

"Phew!" he said. "You don't tell me!"

At the same time, he nodded to Kildare and prompted, "Go on. I'm listening."

"Your syndicate office has immediate access to every means of communication, to several of the radio stations in town, and, of course, to the newspapers, although I'm afraid they'll come out too late to do any good."

"You don't tell me," the chief said. "Right." He slammed up the phone. "And you say Wu Fang is doing this?" he snapped. "You'd swear to it?"

"I'm positive," Kildare assured him.

"Get this," the chief ordered tensely. "Here's something else that one of the boys just phoned in. You know the little ten year old Stuyvesant heiress they've been making so much fuss about lately?"

Kildare nodded.

"She was just found murdered in her playroom," the chief rushed on. "There was a black lotus in her hand."

Hazard gasped and the chief went on.

"Everyone who is in danger tries to get a guard. First thing they do is put a mask or handkerchief over their nose and mouth. All right. What are you and Carson going to do now?"

"We plan to stay and see it through," Kildare said.

"O.K. Fine. Then, Jerry, you run the show. Go back through the issues of the last two months. I'll contact the radio stations and have them cut in on all the programs every five minutes and announce the precautions that you suggested, Kildare. I'll have the switchboard operator hold two lines open constantly."

From then on, things buzzed in the back office where the old papers were filed. Hazard was working like mad. He took the paper of the night before, called a name from the front page. Kildare grabbed a phone directory. Carson had another and they both searched for the number. Then the switchboard operator tried to get it for them.

Hazard was jotting down names, looking them up in the phone book himself. Four or five calls went out—six. Warnings flashed out over the telephone to the individuals, but it was too late! The six were already dead.

The little radio that had been droning away in the office paused, and the voice of the announcer came on.

"We interrupt our program at this point," he said, "to announce a grave crisis. We have just received word from the McNulty News Syndicate that everyone in the city and surrounding country is in danger. Government agent Val Kildare suggests a partial remedy. Everyone, particularly all prominent people, is advised to tie a handkerchief over his nose and mouth so that no poison can touch his lips or nasal passages. This is imperative no matter where you are—in your bedroom, living room, on the street, or any other place. We now turn you back to the program to which you were listening."

Over and over again the warnings were repeated. Every radio station in town was doing its best. Celebrities who had been in the news recently were being warned, and almost as fast as the warning went out, news came back of the deaths of some who had not yet been told of their danger.

Suddenly a wild scream rent the air. Kildare stopped short

and spun around. He turned and stared through the door into the outer office.

"Someone probably got word of the death of a friend or relative," Carson suggested.

"That scream," Kildare shouted, "came from the chief's office." WRITERS AND reporters were rushing toward the door marked "Private" where the great brains of the McNulty Syndicate worked. Someone reached the door before Kildare and threw it open. They stared inside. There the chief leaned back in his chair, his head lolled on the back of it and his mouth open. His hands were locked at his throat and a horrible expression of anguish was frozen on his face.

Kildare drove past the others.

"Get out of here," he cried. "Back, all of you."

And with that, he whirled and drove them out of the office. He slammed the door shut, leaving the rigid form of the chief still inside.

"Quick!" Kildare yelled. "Has anybody got a cane? A club—anything I can use!"

He did see a cane hanging from a hat tree beside a desk.

"Quick!" the government man yelled. "Toss me that cane."

Somebody caught hold of the cane and tossed it to Kildare who caught it expertly. He whirled with his back to the door of the private office and faced the others.

"There's something deadly in there," he said. "An animal, snake, beast or something. I can tell from the way the chief died."

"Died!" came a chorus of several voices.

"Yes, died," Kildare snapped. "And unless we stick together and fight this menace that has come down on us, I wouldn't give a nickel for any life here."

He pointed to the crack under the door.

"That space is large enough for a hundred deadly beasts to come through," he said. "The cause of the chief's death may be out here already. And there will be more than one. Keep back out of the way. The rest of you get anything you can use for clubs. Stand outside this door and if anything comes out, kill it. Don't take the slightest chance!"

Hazard and Carson took their cue. Already they were standing by the door, Carson with someone's heavy umbrella in his hand and Hazard on the other side with a bar of lead from the press room.

"O.K.," Kildare said. "Now watch out. I'm going in."

With a quick move, Kildare threw open the door, slid in, and closed it after him.

Hazard could see the government man's shadow against the panes of frosted glass, darting and ducking about. He could hear his swift breathing and the rap of the cane as it came down on the floor or smacked against the wall.

Something came wriggling under the door like a small black bolt of lightning. It was a tiny, deadly snake!

Bam! Bam! Bam!

Clubs of every description clouted the floor. Carson caught the snake with the head of his umbrella and crushed it with his heel. Hazard leaped back beside the door again, for the banging continued inside the private office.

123

Then the glass door of the private office splintered, and Kildare shouted.

"Look out! It's coming out there!"

Hazard, who was nearest, leaped to the door. There, poised on the glass, was a weird little beast. It resembled a tiny cat, but the nose was pointed like that of a rat and the legs were long. It was dull brown in color and its back was scaled.

Hazard leaped away, trying to dodge the little beast, but the demon thing landed on his right arm and its claws dug into his flesh.

Hazard tried to switch the lead bar from his right hand to his left so he could hit the beast, but at that moment something swept through the air and struck his arm a stunning blow.

Wham!

As the head of Carson's umbrella connected with the ghastly little beast, it flattened, clung for a moment, then dropped to the floor. Hazard, panting and breathless, spun around and tried to lift the lead bar to finish the deadly thing, but his arm was numb and he couldn't move it.

Wham! Wham!

Carson struck twice. The beast was badly injured but it leaped at him with a speed that was amazing. Carson darted back and kicked at it with his feet. The beast sprawled for an instant and Hazard, with all the fury born of desperation, leaped into the air and came down with both feet on the creature. There was a high-pitched squawk, and then the deadly little beast lay twitching on the floor.

A cry came from the front of the office. Members of the

staff, writers and reporters, were pounding the floor in front of the office door. A snake no larger than a lead pencil was wriggling between their blows, fairly leaping from the floor.

Someone yelled in sudden agony. A tiny animal, moving so fast that they could barely distinguish it, shot through the air, landed on the victim's foot and vanished up his trouser leg. A sudden stiffening of his body, and the syndicate reporter toppled over backward and crashed to the floor.

A FAST-TRAVELING beast that resembled a tiny lizard was dodging the blows in front of the door. Hazard, who had succeeded in picking up the lead bar with his left hand—his right was still numb from the terrific blow of Carson's umbrella—aimed at the lizard and struck again and again, but he wasn't accurate with that hand.

"Spread out!" Carson yelled. "Spread out! If we miss these beasts as they come out of the door, the rest of you will have to get them."

"Kildare!" Hazard cried. "You'd better come out now. We can get them as they come under the door!"

"Watch the broken glass," Kildare yelled. "One has already gone through it. We can't get them all."

Hazard leaped around to the side.

"Come on," he yelled to Kildare. "You can't keep it up in there. You—"

He broke off and swung with all his might at a beast slightly larger than a rat that leaped at him from the edge of the jagged glass. There was a squeal of rage and pain as the lead bar connected, and the body of the little death beast was hurled through the air and flattened against the side of a desk.

Something sprang at him from the shadow of another desk. Panic put wings to his feet and he leaped clear. But the hideous cat-like thing started to spring again.

A scream came from another part of the room, followed by a horrible, gurgling sound. Someone else was gone. From the office there came the bellow of Kildare's automatic.

Blam! Blam! Blam!

From just outside came the high-pitched scream of a beast. Or was it the scream of a human in mortal terror? Hazard heard the door of the private office swing open and slam shut again and he knew Kildare was among them. The government man was batting the floor in front of the door with the end of the cane.

"Get around to the side and help Jerry!" he shouted to Carson. "There will be more coming through the broken pane of glass. I'll take care of this end."

The fighting went on, as the awful beasts continued to pour from that horror-packed private office.

Two more writers screamed and fell as the beasts of that yellow devil, Wu Fang, attacked them.

"Somebody call the police!" Kildare yelled.

A half dozen phones clicked with frantic hands banging their hooks, but their means of communication were completely cut off, and just at that moment every light in the place went out. Except for the dim glow reflected from the street lights, they were plunged into total darkness.

"We can't get anyone," came the panic-stricken voices of those who had tried the phones. "The phones are all dead. All the cables leading into this place have been cut."

CHAPTER 13
THE BLACK TOMB

IN THE next instant, Kildare's flash light flared. Someone screamed, and again there was that abrupt muffling of the sound as another victim met sudden and awful death.

"Light the papers in the wastebaskets!" Kildare yelled.

Half a dozen lights flared as the contents of metal wastebaskets were ignited.

The feeling had returned to Hazard's arm and he took out a match with his right hand and kicked a wastepaper basket from under a desk. Something leaped at him out of the blackness. He struck it a glancing blow and knocked it to the floor. Then flames were licking up from several wastebaskets, lighting the room in a weird glow of flickering fire.

The place was in a wild uproar. People were screaming and falling to the floor dead. Windows crashed on every side and there, silhouetted on the sills, were weird misshapen forms that might be half man, half beast.

Hazard froze for an instant as he stared at a window just beside him. There was a ghastly-looking, hairy shape that stood out against the lights of the city beyond. A hairy shape with a flat head and long legs on a short, stubby body, and short, very powerful arms.

The ghastly man-beast glared in at him with eyes that seemed to glow, and he pounded the glass pane with his fist until he smashed it in. He climbed through, and instinctively, Hazard reached for his gun. Then he remembered that he had left it with Mohra. He was desperate.

"Kildare!" he cried. "Look! Get that thing."

He knew they had guns, but the din was so great that Jerry Hazard could scarcely hear his own voice. He shifted the lead bar to his right hand. Yes, he was sure he could use it now.

The long, powerful legs of the man-beast bent and he sprang at Hazard. The newspaper man tried to duck, but the figure was coming with incredible speed. The weight of the hairy, stinking body crashed full against him with its stubby arms outstretched.

Hazard cried out as he felt the hands grasp his shoulders and the fingers bite deeply into his flesh as he and the beast fell to the floor.

Hazard was trying to wriggle out from under the foul-smelling thing. Suddenly, the long legs of the beast were about his own, squeezing, pressing with terrific force, and the hands were moving slowly across his shoulders toward his throat.

The evil, flat-headed face that was almost completely covered with hair was leering at him. Great tusked teeth were bared and the eyes were glowing again with that fanatic gleam. A cackling laugh came from the ugly open mouth.

Hazard felt the fingers close about his throat. He was powerless to move but he managed to cry out for help. Where were Carson and Kildare? Had the beasts got them? There was still a thunderous roar of clubs beating about the room, and shouts rent the air as some of the people were attacked by the poisonous beasts.

Then above him and to the left he heard a cry. Two shots rang out in quick succession.

Blam! Blam!

The man-beast screamed in pain and fear, and the grotesque body rolled away from him.

"We've got to get out of here!" he heard Kildare yell. "Jerry, where are you?"

Hazard knew then that it had been Carson's gun that had saved him, for Kildare's voice came from the other side of the room. Hazard could hear him more clearly now because the din had subsided somewhat.

"Jerry! Jerry! Where are you?"

Hazard was on his feet, trying his best to say something, struggling to answer Kildare. His hands were at his throat and for the moment he seemed to be able to do nothing but gasp and gulp for breath.

Finally, he managed to choke out, "I'm here, Kildare."

The government man was coming toward him. He could see him dimly through the mass of disordered desks and chairs.

"Do you know a back way out of here, Jerry?" Kildare was shouting.

Then he paused as he saw Hazard stagger. A news hound standing close to Hazard cut in with, "I'll show you the way. Come on. Out the back door."

Carson had Hazard's arm and was steadying him.

"Come on, old man," he encouraged. "You'll make it."

The ghostly figure marched deliberately towards them.

There was a general rush for the door by those who still lived. They charged down the stairs in the wake of the newspaper man who had volunteered to show them the way. There was the sound of a metal door opening and then a terrific scream.

"Down everybody!" Kildare yelled.

Hazard was behind the government man and he couldn't see what was going on. There were other screams down in front and the blasting of Kildare's automatic. They charged on.

"Carson!" Kildare shouted. "Come on with your guns! Keep your nose and your mouth covered!"

Blam! Blam! Blam!

Automatics bucked and chattered and there were cries from out in the courtyard behind the building. Hazard couldn't see what Kildare and Carson were shooting at but he was right behind them, staggering, trying to keep his feet.

"Come on!" Kildare cried. "This way!"

AS THEY raced out across the dark court, Kildare stumbled over a body, caught himself, and lunged on. Hazard was following Kildare's directions, holding his hand over his mouth as he ran. They broke through a yard at the back of the court and raced out onto another street. They heard the sound of fire sirens but there wasn't time to pay any attention to that.

Kildare rushed immediately to the curb and whistled shrilly for a cab. One swerved over toward them and they piled in, all three of them panting desperately from the terrific struggle they had been through.

Kildare turned to Carson and said, "You've got two guns, Rod. Give one to Hazard. We'll probably need them."

There was a grim, determined look on Val Kildare's face that Hazard had seen only a few times before, and when that expression had appeared Kildare had always forced the issue.

"This time," the government man said softly, "we're going to get Wu Fang. But we've got to get Wong Chu out of jail first, and we're going to do that if we have to hold up the whole police force."

"I don't think there will be many there at headquarters to stop us," Carson ventured.

"No," Kildare said, "that's what I'm counting on. Get your guns loaded."

The cab stopped in front of headquarters and the three men piled out and ran up the steps. Inside, Hazard stared in sudden amazement, for this wasn't at all what he had expected.

The office was empty. Val Kildare called out but his voice simply echoed through the room. They strode back to the captain's desk but there was no one there. Then suddenly, Kildare tensed.

"Wait a minute," he said. "What's that?"

Hazard could hear very faintly the sound of shouting. It was muffled and came from another room. Kildare turned slowly until he located the direction from which it came, then he strode toward a closed door at the left of the room. The three stopped outside the door for a moment and listened. They heard voices— the voice of an oriental, husky and pleading, and deep, bellowing American voices.

"I tell you the Chang Li has nothing to do with it. That is all I can say."

133

An angry voice snapped back at the oriental, "You dirty, lying little yellow rat. I'm going to get the truth out of you if I have to kill you with this whip."

Kildare's hand was on the door and he flung it open and charged in, followed by Carson and Hazard. Except for a few chairs, the room was bare of furnishings. A bright overhead light shot its powerful beam straight down into the face of a frightened yellow man. It was Wong Chu. He was stripped to the waist and bound securely to a chair. A man in civilian clothes stood in front of him with a whip raised over his head. In the next second it would come down on the bare flesh of the Chinese.

The Chinaman stared up pleadingly. Already there were red welts on his flesh where the whip had bitten into his body. But that whip never landed again, for a sharp command from Val Kildare stopped it half way down on its mission of torture.

"Freeze where you are or I'll fill you with lead," the government man snapped.

Not a soul in that room moved. There were other lights, and Kildare seemed to know where the switch was, for he snapped them on without taking his eyes off the man before him.

Now they saw that there were three police officers in the room besides the man with the whip in his hand. They all turned and stared, their faces drawn and tense.

"Go around to the side so that you don't get into my line of fire," Kildare ordered, jerking his head to Hazard, "and turn out that powerful light that's burning out Wong Chu's eyes."

Hazard obeyed, went around so that he was in the center of

134

the group. He reached the powerful, shaded light and switched it off.

Wong Chu looked up and blinked. He nodded at Hazard and Kildare.

"I shall never forget this," he said sincerely.

One of the police officers started to speak, but Kildare cut him off with a sharp, "Shut up. If I've got to take command of this outfit to see that justice is done, I'll give the orders. Jerry, stand back and cover these birds. Carson, you go over to the side."

Carson and Hazard took their positions as the government man ordered. Kildare began to speak once more but one of the police officers cut him off. Hazard saw now that he was one of the chief inspectors.

"For the love of heaven," he said in a voice that was pleading, "you don't realize what's going on."

"Oh, don't I?" Kildare retorted. "What do you think we've been doing in the McNulty Syndicate office? We've been warning all the people we could to protect themselves."

"No, no," the inspector said. "That isn't what I mean. You don't realize how serious this is. Washington has received a demand from Wu Fang, in the name of the Chang Li, to turn over this entire country to him. He threatens to kill every living inhabitant with his poisons and his beasts. And this little rat"—he nodded to Wong Chu—"is the head of the Chang Li but we can't get a thing out of him."

"You're crazy," Kildare snapped. "Don't you realize what's happening? Wu Fang is behind the whole thing. I could have explained that this morning to you and your men but you wouldn't have listened. I'm telling you now, but I don't care whether you listen or not. We're running this show from now on and we're not taking any chances on interference from you."

The government man nodded to the chief inspector.

"Untie Wong Chu," he ordered.

The inspector hesitated.

"But don't you realize," he protested, "that the whole country is in danger? He's going to murder the entire population in every city if the government doesn't surrender the treasury to him at once."

Kildare's gun moved significantly and he said sternly, "I told you to untie Wong Chu, Inspector. I repeat it, but that's the last time I'm going to say it."

The inspector moved quickly to the back of the Chinaman's chair and cut the ropes without any further argument. Wong Chu got up.

"Now help him put his clothes on," Kildare ordered. "Hurry!"

Wong Chu's shirt and coat were lying on another chair at the side of the room. The chief inspector picked them up and handed them to him.

"You're going to be sorry for this, Kildare," he growled. "This is a serious offense."

Kildare shrugged.

"Are you ready, Wong Chu?"

Wong Chu bowed.

"Yes," honorable Mr. Kildare," he said, "I am ready. We go to place I mention?"

"RIGHT," THE government man nodded. He jerked his head to Carson and Hazard. Together, they backed out of the door, leaving the police inspectors gaping in amazement. Kildare locked the door from the outside.

"That will hold them a minute or two," he said. "Come on!" He took Wong Chu by the arm.

They were outside, running down the steps, piling into a cab.

"I don't see how you expect to find Wu Fang on a night like this when all these murders are coming off. He'll be outside somewhere, running the show, won't he?"

Wong Chu shook his head.

"I do not think so," he said. "I believe I can show you where Wu Fang is. You are not afraid?"

"Afraid?" Kildare demanded. "After what we've just been through?"

"I mean you are not afraid of evil spirits," Wong Chu corrected. "They say that the little cemetery is haunted. People do not go there at night. Perhaps it is because the secret entrance to Wu Fang's new hiding place is in that cemetery."

"You mean the graveyard at the edge of Chinatown, the one that runs along one side of the little church?" Kildare asked.

Wong Chu nodded quickly.

"That is correct, Mr. Kildare," he said gravely. "I will show you." He leaned forward to the cab driver and ordered him to draw up to the curb. "I take this opportunity of leaving the car," Wong Chu explained, "so that we may walk to the cemetery. It will be a little safer, I believe."

They turned into the ancient graveyard where flowers and

shrubs mingled with the tombstones. It was very dark and they had to pick their way cautiously. A high stone wall surrounded the two sides of the cemetery, shutting it off from the alleys and buildings beyond.

They had gone perhaps twenty or thirty feet inside the low wall that separated the cemetery from the sidewalk when Wong Chu hesitated for a moment.

"I would advise walking very softly," he said. "We do not want to let Wu Fang know that we are coming. It must be a complete surprise in order to be successful."

Suddenly, Hazard saw Kildare tense and clutch Wong Chu's arm. The Chinaman stopped talked instantly. Then the newspaper man saw what had attracted Kildare's attention.

There was something white beyond a clump of shrubbery to the left, less than five feet away. It moved, but there seemed to be no sound. Then the white figure ran down along the side of the cemetery wall, darting with nymph-like skill from shrub to shrub.

Kildare brought out his flash light and turned it on. But now the white form was gone. He leaped forward and raced for the spot where the ghostly apparition had vanished.

Hazard followed as fast as he could, passing Wong Chu in his dash across the graves. He reached Kildare's side as the government man bent over a marble slab laid in the ground. He looked about in a bewildered fashion.

"That's funny," he said in a low voice. "I'd have sworn that figure came this way. I know it stopped right here. It disappeared behind this headstone, and the only place it could have gone is down in this grave under the marble slab."

He bent down again. "Come on," he said. "Give me a hand."

An eerie feeling came over Jerry Hazard as his fingers clutched the edge of the stone slab. It was clammy and cold to his touch. Carson got his fingers in the crack and pulled, but the stone didn't budge. After several futile attempts, they straightened and Kildare shook his head. "I can't believe it," he said. "Whoever was in this graveyard is under that slab of marble. It must be some kind of a door that's locked from the inside."

"Perhaps it was a ghost," Wong Chu suggested. "In that case, it would not have to lift up the slab."

"That was no ghost," Kildare assured him. "That was a girl dressed in a light, filmy gown."

A girl! Carson and Hazard gasped in amazement and Carson uttered the name that was uppermost in his mind at the time.

"You mean it might be—Tanya?" he demanded.

Kildare shrugged.

"I don't know," he said. "I couldn't see her plainly enough to be sure. But it was a girl, all right. I'm sure she went down under that slab of stone. There may be some other place for her to go after she gets into the grave."

He straightened and turned to Wong Chu.

"There doesn't seem to be anything we can do about it at the present time," he said. "Where do we go from here, Wong Chu?"

The Chinaman nodded and said, "Come. I will show you."

He led them on toward the rear of the church. There he

turned the corner of the ancient stone and progressed to the right.

Suddenly, all four of them stopped as a weird, eerie sound came from somewhere. It was a low moan, like the sound of wind blowing through the branches of a pine tree. And still Hazard had a feeling that the moan came from a human throat.

In the center of the rear section of the cemetery was a black marble structure that measured perhaps fifteen feet across the front and a little less in depth. It was black, and it appeared now as though these gaunt tombstones were guarding it.

Wong Chu raised his hand with a slow, dignified gesture and pointed to the dark, shadowy mausoleum before them.

In a low, tense voice, he said, "The entrance to Wu Fang's hiding place is through the Black Tomb."

CHAPTER 14
THE HAVEN OF HORROR

AGAIN THE low, moaning sound came, and this time it was apparent that it issued from the entrance to the Black Tomb. The four men stood twenty feet away from it and no one moved forward. Even Kildare seemed to be waiting and watching for something.

Suddenly there was a creak of rusty hinges, and the iron-barred door that served as an entrance to the tomb was opening slowly, inch by inch. The creaking continued.

Now the door was open wide, but they could see nothing but a black void inside. Then slowly, in that black space, a figure took shape—a small figure coming slowly out of the Black Tomb. It looked like a little girl of about twelve years of age.

Yes, it was a girl, but not a white girl. She was Chinese and she was walking very slowly toward them with deliberate, measured steps. Her hands were out in front of her like the groping hands of a person walking in his sleep. She moaned as she came nearer.

Suddenly, Kildare hissed, "Nee-Sa, you little she-devil, what are you doing here? If you think you can scare us with this sort of foolishness, you're crazy."

Kildare's gun was out now and he had it leveled at the girl. Now Nee-Sa spoke.

"I am not here to frighten you," she assured them. "It would be foolish for a little girl like me to try to scare big, strong men like you. I am here to warn you that you can not carry out this mission that you are on. You must not enter the Black Tomb!"

"Nee-Sa," Kildare hissed, "if you make one false move to get back to Wu Fang and tell him that we're here, I'll kill you just as sure as my finger is on the trigger."

And then in the darkness a horrible thing happened. He heard Nee-Sa laugh, a childish, derisive little gurgle.

"You can not kill me, Mr. Kildare," she said. "For if you did, Wu Fang would surely hear the report of the gun and he would know then that you were coming. Anyway"—the little she-devil laughed again, like a delighted child at play—"you can not kill evil spirits."

Then, directly in front of them, a wall of white vapor suddenly shot up with a puffing sound and obliterated Nee-Sa from their sight. Kildare plunged through the white cloud, groping wildly. He had no more than touched the white veil when it vanished, and they were alone. Nee-Sa had disappeared.

Kildare gasped as his eyes glimpsed something in the air above them and to the left. Huge black wings were flapping up there—something was flying. A giant black bat had taken off, right out of the white vapor where Nee-Sa had been a moment before, and now it was flying over the high stone wall at the back of the cemetery.

Hazard's blood chilled. There was no explanation for it so far as he could see. He had read fairy tales of things like this, yarns that the witches spun about beautiful girls turning into dragons and bats. But this was different; he had seen this with his own eyes. The newspaper man was frozen with astonishment and awe, realizing only dimly that other things were going on about him.

Wong Chu breathed, "It's the black bat from the Black Tomb."

Carson uttered a low curse of astonishment.

Kildare was lunging forward, flash light in his hand, plunging into the tomb of black marble. After a long, tense moment, his voice came to them reassuringly.

"Come on in," he hissed. "There's nothing to be afraid of."

Gingerly, Hazard followed Kildare, but he could think of a great many things he would rather be doing at the moment. His thoughts flashed back to Mohra? Was she still safe in the apartment with the cops guarding her? He recalled the terrible moments in the syndicate office and the wholesale killings.

How could he feel that Mohra was safe when those ghastly, unbelievable things had happened?

But there was no time to turn back now. He must go on with the others and finish Wu Fang, for only when that had been accomplished could he and Mohra be together again.

It was comforting, as he peered into the tomb entrance, to see the light of Kildare's electric torch playing about the place. It took away some of the weird, chilling atmosphere.

"That's funny," the government man was saying. "There's no other door out of this place, and Nee-Sa is gone. She couldn't possibly have dodged around either corner of the building, because I was watching for that. That puff of smoke or vapor was just large enough to cover her movements for a moment."

"You do not believe that she changed into the black bat?" Wong Chu asked.

Kildare shook his head.

No," he said, "no one could ever make me believe that. That was simply to draw our attention while she made her getaway. Don't ask me how it was done, for that's only one of the many unexplainable things that Wu Fang has at his command. Well, where do we go from here?"

Wong Chu hesitated.

"It is said," he repeated, "that the entrance to Wu Fang's hiding place is through Joshua Pratt."

With that, the Chinese leader of the Chang Li began staring about the inside of the marble tomb. It had apparently been built many years before by a wealthy family who could afford black marble. The family must have been quite large, for there was a passageway, perhaps three feet wide, extending down the center of the mausoleum from front to rear, and on each side were spaces where full-length marble slabs marked the final resting places of the individual members.

Wong Chu held out his hand and Hazard noticed that it trembled a little, but the Chinaman's voice was steady as he said, "May I borrow your flash light, Mr. Kildare?"

The government man handed it to him and now, with the beam traveling in front of him, Wong Chu began inspecting the inscriptions on the various tombs. He read them aloud.

"Mary Anna Witherspoon." He passed on to the next and read, "Katherine Pratt." He inspected the rest of the six tombs on that side of the aisle without finding what he sought. Now he started down the other side.

"John Pratt," he read. "Katy Weeder."

He stopped at the next one, pointed to the inscription, and read, "Joshua Pratt, born 1806, died 1889."

"I don't get it," Carson said, snaking his head.

"It is said," Wong Chu repeated, "that the entrance to Wu Fang's hiding place is through Joshua Pratt."

"Of course," Kildare nodded. "Don't you understand, Rod? Wu Fang has had a passage made through the place where Joshua Pratt's body once lay. Here, give me a hand."

He bent down and thrust his fingers under the marble slab.

"That's funny," he said. "It doesn't move. This ought to come up like a trap door."

"That was my understanding," Wong Chu said.

"Come on, Jerry and Rod," Kildare said. "Give me a hand here."

The two bent down to help Kildare. They strained and tugged but the marble slab remained immovable. Suddenly, Kildare straightened and stared down at the slab.

"I think I have it," he said. "I'll put my foot on it and see what happens."

He stepped on the slab with one foot. It gave away under his foot, tipped down on one side.

"**THAT'S IT,**" he said. "A mighty clever device. I'll gamble that's the way the marble slab in the other grave worked. It's a trap door all right but it opens down instead of up. Wait now. Let's see if I'm right. We'll find out how quickly a person could vanish under here. In all probability, Wu Fang's agents would want to get away and disappear underground quicker than they would want to come up. Stand aside and I'll try it"

The three stepped back. Wong Chu was still holding the flash light as Kildare walked over to the door of the tomb. Now the government man came in on a trot.

"Watch this," he said as he neared the marble slab under which once had rested the body of Joshua Pratt. "I may need some help."

He threw his body across the marble slab much as a baseball player might slide to a base. Without a sound the slab gave way under him, dropped him down easily. They saw him slip from sight into a dark void. Instantly, the marble slab came up in place again, held by a strong spring.

145

Hazard was suddenly filled with apprehension; he leaped forward and cried, "Kildare, are you all right? Are you hurt?"

He waited a moment and then Kildare's answer came, "Yes, I'm O.K. Come on down."

He pulled the marble slab so that it turned down and peered up through the opening. They could see that he was kneeling below.

"I'll hold it back while the rest of you come down," he said.

Hazard was the first to enter the opening. To his astonishment, his knees came in contact with a carpet, thick and soft and noise-deadening. He moved back of Kildare into a narrow passage that went down four or five steps until they could stand erect.

"There," Kildare said. "At last we're inside. Are the rest of you down?"

"Right," Carson replied.

"We are with you," Wong Chu said. "Now I will try to lead you through the passages to Wu Fang, may his ancestors have mercy on him."

Wong Chu led them down a corridor that was so narrow their shoulders touched in places. But this corridor was different from others that Hazard had used in Chinatown. They had been musty, weird, and damp, but this passage that they were in now had a carpeted floor and heavy draperies over the ceiling and side walls. The sweet fragrance of an oriental perfume filled the air. This was truly a passage fit for a great ruler, a lord of crime.

"And so this leads us to the place from which Wu Fang has

issued his orders to the United States government," Carson ventured.

"That is what we trust," Wong Chu hissed back.

"I am sure of my direction," Kildare whispered. "We're traveling straight into Chinatown. No one would ever think of looking for the entrance to Wu Fang's place in a cemetery."

A muffled sound came to them from just ahead, then something fluttered through the air. The rays of the flash light that Wong Chu held caught a tiny white thing beating against the ceiling of the passage. But before they could reach it, it vanished behind one of the drapes.

"Watch out for a sudden attack from that white bat," Kildare warned. "It might be one of those from the suicide tomb."

They passed on. There was little need of a guide now, for the passage was one long, single hall without any corridors branching off. They came to a place where the passage widened and found themselves in a fair-sized, well-lighted room. Across it, they could see where the passage led on.

They were all inside the chamber when suddenly, with a dull thud, the passage ahead was completely blocked. Wong Chu stopped, but Kildare leaped ahead and grabbed the light out of his hand.

"Come on!" the government man cried. He whirled around and dashed to the other end of the room through which they had entered.

Thud!

Another dull sound and drapes suddenly swung over in front

of that passage. Hazard had a panicky feeling that behind those curtains was a solid door or wall that could not be penetrated.

Kildare was pounding on it frantically, trying to find a way of opening it. He turned back and tried the other side. Hazard, Carson, and Wong Chu were traveling around the edge of the room, trying desperately to find an opening.

A sudden panic seized Hazard and it didn't help any when Kildare spoke, putting all their fears into words as he said, "We're trapped. We're caught in this room. Every exit is closed and fastened tightly, but we may as well keep calm because it won't help to get excited."

CHAPTER 15
THE TORTURE DEATH

VAL KILDARE turned off his light and they were plunged into utter darkness.

"Anyone else got a flash light?" he asked.

No one answered.

"But we have three automatics," Kildare went on. "Have you anything you could use in a fight, Wong Chu?" he asked.

"I regret to say, Mr. Kildare, that I have nothing. Everything was taken from me at police headquarters."

"Then we have one flash light, probably a few matches, and three automatics. Have you any idea what Wu Fang is planning, Wong Chu?"

"You mean," Wong Chu asked, "that Wu Fang knows we are coming? He is planning for our capture?"

"What else would you think?" Kildare asked.

"I am hoping, honorable Mr. Kildare," Wong Chu said, "that Wu Fang does not know yet of our coming; that the black bat was Nee-Sa, the Chinese girl, in another form. Perhaps we can still surprise him. We may have trapped ourselves in here by stepping on a portion of the floor which closed the doors when we entered."

Hazard's heart was pounding like mad with a frantic hope. Perhaps Wong Chu was right! Perhaps Wu Fang didn't know of their presence! His hopes fell again as he caught the expression of calm resignation of Kildare's face. It was easy to tell that he wasn't placing much faith in the belief that Wu Fang didn't know they were there.

"At any rate," Kildare said, "we'll try that idea. Perhaps we can step on some portion of the floor that will open the doors again."

"Yes," Wong Chu said, "I would suggest that we try."

There was a fanatic eagerness in Jerry Hazard's movements as he helped in that hunt. Before he was through, he had tramped over every section of the floor in the room. They met in the center again, and Kildare turned out his light to save the battery while they talked in the inky blackness.

"I guess that's out," the government man said. "We've searched the side walls and the floor throughout without finding anything that will open the doors. We can't do a thing—not until we're sent for."

"Sent for!" Wong Chu echoed hollowly. "You mean then that you are sure Wu Fang has trapped us here deliberately?"

"Yes," Kildare said, "I'm positive. There's no use in fooling ourselves any longer."

At that, the government man left the little group in the center of the room. Hazard could hear his feet as he paced the floor a little way off. The number one government man was trying to think—trying to devise a plan. Would he succeed? Hazard was wondering, hoping, praying that he could, for that would be their only salvation.

And what of Mohra? His mind flashed back to her constantly and a half-insane rage surged over him at his helplessness.

Suddenly, there was a cry from Kildare. It was muffled and choking and he said something that sounded like "Help!" His flash light dropped to the floor as something creaked and banged.

Jerry Hazard lunged forward in the darkness, gun in hand, with Carson beside him. They groped frantically, ran into each other. They separated, found the corner of the room from which Kildare's voice had come and lunged against the hard wall. But Kildare was not there. He was gone!

Hazard's foot kicked something that made a clattering sound. He reached down and groped about on the floor. His heart leaped as his hand touched Kildare's flash light. Eagerly, he switched it on, but there was no light. The bulb must have been broken in the fall.

A muffled gasp came from the other side of the room. Then they heard Wong Chu's voice knife through the darkness.

"Mr. Kildare! Help! I—"

Then all sound of his voice was choked off as Hazard and Carson lunged to the other side of the room. Wild panic seized the newspaper man. He wanted to shoot, but dared not for fear of hitting Wong Chu. They reached the other side of the room in a mad rush, but their out stretched hands met nothing.

Something clutched Hazard's arm—a groping, grasping smelly thing. Instantly, Hazard whirled, flung his other hand on his arm. It fell on a great, hairy forearm, brutally powerful. Strong fingers bit cruelly into his flesh. That surely wasn't Wong Chu.

His right arm with the gun in it came spinning around and his fingers were flexing the trigger.

Blam! Blam! Blam!

The automatic barked, and in the flashes, Hazard could see a heavy squat figure. Carson cried out and then his gun exploded. In the next instant, the interior of the room was full of fighting, tearing, stinking half savages.

Hazard was yelling to Carson, "Quick! Back to back! It's our only chance! We've got to fight it out."

But Carson didn't even hear him, or if he did he gave no answer. Hazard sensed with a shudder that he was alone with the horrible man-beasts of the Dragon Lord of Crime and the Emperor of Death. Insane rage and desperation seized him. He scarcely realized what was going on or what he was doing. Men were attacking him from every side. Something was hurled at his head, but it missed its mark and struck his shoulder. His left arm went numb.

HAZARD STILL clutched the automatic in his right hand and he was standing now in the middle of the room, turning as fast as he could and shooting straight out from him as the

151

men came. The room was filled with a bedlam of sound—screams of death—cries of terror and pain.

Suddenly, the gun was empty. Hazard tried to move his left arm, found that some feeling had returned to it. He struck with it at a hairy figure that he felt clawing for his throat, and managed to push his attacker away.

Then he stumbled over dead and writhing bodies on the floor and fell backward on a still form. He must have landed on the back or chest of the body, for there was a grunt and an outward puff of air—the last that those lungs would ever exhale.

That was a lucky thing for Hazard. As he lay there, he could hear the grunts and sodden thuds that told him the agents of Wu Fang were fighting among themselves, each thinking the other was Hazard.

The newspaper man found another clip of cartridges in his pocket and shot it into the automatic handle. But he suddenly thought that more shots from him would let the agents know where he was. It would be better if he crawled along the floor silently.

With heart pounding and taut nerves ready to snap, he started off in the darkness. He had no sense of direction, and everything was still pitch dark. A body hurled over him. Someone stepped on his leg. Another foot tramped on his hand. He crawled over dead bodies and bodies that he could feel still twitching in the last throes of death.

He reached a wall and began following it, pulling the drapes back and crawling behind them. He came to an opening in the wall through which a dim light shone. Now was his chance.

Perhaps this would lead into the chamber where they had taken Wong Chu and Carson and Kildare. Would they still be alive when he reached them?

Two half-naked, stinking figures came running out of the chamber toward the opening. Hazard dropped in a heap to the floor and buried his head in the crook of his arm. They passed by and he again crawled on.

He found himself in a passage wide enough for two men to walk abreast and got to his feet. No use crawling any longer. Where would this passage lead? Those two men who had been trying to capture him had gone this way. He followed with his gun cocked and his finger on the trigger.

Hazard was walking rapidly. He limped now and his left arm was partially paralyzed. Someone was running behind him. There was a dim light shining at the other end of the corridor, and he realized that he must not let the other figure catch up with him and see him. He didn't dare shoot, because that would warn whoever was at the other end of the passage.

Hazard found himself running now to keep ahead of that pursuing figure. He heard the other shout. The warning was out. Realizing that there was no longer any use to try to keep his presence here in the corridor a secret, Hazard spun around and ran backward, shooting from the hip.

As the Chinaman behind pitched over in the corridor, and sprawled on his face, Hazard turned to race on, but something happened to block his plans at that moment. He never was quite sure what it was. It might have been a step that he hadn't seen. At any rate, as he turned from his backward run, his feet caught and he fell, struggling frantically to catch himself.

Something flashed in front of his face, and he realized that it must be a club, swung from behind one of the drapes at the side of the passage.

Wham!

It struck his gun wrist and his whole arm went numb. He didn't know where the gun had gone, but tried desperately with his left hand to find it. Then it seemed to him, in the few moments that followed, that there were a hundred brown and yellow skinned natives beating him with clubs and sticks.

But in spite of that, Jerry Hazard got to his feet. His fists were flying, smacking bodies and faces in the narrow corridor. It was his last stand and he knew it. He would make the best of it while he had the chance.

Brown and yellow men went down before his savage struggling, but others came in to replace them. His opponents began to grow dim before his eyes and the next thing he realized was that he was being dragged down the corridor by a group of babbling yellow men.

Hazard could scarcely move. He tried once to coil his legs to get a footing, but it wouldn't work. Two yellow beasts had him by the wrists, and he was aware of a terrific pain in his right arm where the club had struck him.

They hurried him on down the stairs, then suddenly he was in a large, brightly-lighted room, filled with the odor of incense. He could hear a soft voice that was very familiar to him.

"Ah, so they have caught you at last, Mr. Hazard," the voice said. It was Wu Fang, Dragon Lord of Crime.

Hazard could scarcely look up, could not answer—didn't seem to care.

"I have the rest of your friends here as my guests," the yellow fiend continued. "It is indeed an honor, gentlemen. And now we will proceed with the little festival I have planned for you. Each of you will entertain those who still remain alive."

THINGS WERE growing a little clearer to Hazard, but his mind was still dulled by the terrific pain. His whole body was growing numb. He saw Wu Fang motion to the yellow beasts who dragged him, and point to braces in a wall or a thick supporting pillar. He couldn't be sure which it was because the drapes were so heavy and confusing.

He noticed that Kildare and Carson were bound to other braces or rings behind them.

Wu Fang turned now and pointed to a strange-looking wooden structure as his agents bound Hazard beside his friends.

"You know what this is, of course, gentlemen," he said.

"You yellow devil," Kildare snapped, "if you use that torture rack—"

Suddenly a great brown-skinned, half-naked Malayan struck Kildare a terrific blow across the mouth, cutting off the government man's words. Kildare's head sagged on his neck for a moment and his eyes glazed. Then he drew himself up straight again.

Wu Fang was smiling with fiendish contentment, and his words were soft and caressing as he said, "Yes, gentlemen, of course that is the correct answer. It is a torture rack. You see—" he pointed to two round bars of wood, one at the top and one at the bottom of the rack. Each had handles sticking from one end. The rack itself was made of heavy wood and placed on an incline of about sixty degrees. Two ropes extended from the winding bar at the top down to the middle of the rack and two more were laid up over some of the supports from the bottom bar.

"Permit me to explain," Wu Fang said. "You see, each of you in turn will be placed on the rack. Your wrists will be bound by the two ropes that hang from the lower bar, then your legs will be fastened to the ropes of the upper."

The yellow fiend pointed to two of his half-naked servants.

"Then my two very strong aides will begin to draw you apart," Wu Fang continued. "Very slowly, your arms and legs will be pulled from their sockets."

Kildare and Carson were struggling like mad to get free, hurling threats at Wu Fang. The yellow fiend held up his hand and smiled again in that devilishly benign manner that was characteristic of him.

"Ah, but wait, honorable gentlemen," he said in a soft tone. "I have not told you all! The most interesting part of the ceremony comes when you are being stretched on the rack and your joints have not quite been pulled apart. During that time another one of my servants will use this little instrument."

Hazard's bulging, blood-shot eyes saw the Emperor of Death pick up a queer implement. It resembled a floor brush and was formed of a block of wood with a handle attached. On the bottom of the block of wood, sharp spikes extended, slanting back a little.

"This instrument," Wu Fang explained with obvious delight, "is used like a rake. Your flesh will be bared before you are placed on the rack, and then, as you are very slowly pulled apart, my third assistant"—he nodded to a yellow beast who was grinning at one side of the rack—"will rake you with this spiked brush. That, my friends, is to help you on your journey into your heaven. It will open your flesh so that the bad spirits may go out before you die. You see, I have a very bad reputation, I am supposed to be cold-hearted and ruthless in my killings, but surely you can not deny that this action is lenient. You see, honorable gentlemen, I have your comfort in the future world under consideration—regardless of what occurs here below."

The Dragon Lord of Crime had finished his speech and now whirled around suddenly. Hazard was staring at him with bulging eyes, his muscles taut. After his speech, all his aches and pains and numbness were nothing.

"Now let me see," Wu Fang said thoughtfully, staring about. "Wong Chu, I believe you have been one of my greatest enemies, for you are one of my kind. You are the member of the Chang Li who was to blame for my excommunication from the organization. Therefore, I will give you the honor of being the first to pass into the land of eternity."

Wu Fang nodded shortly to his aides. Two men leaped forward, seized Wong Chu. The little Chinaman screamed with terror and fought to get free, but he was powerless in the grasp of Wu Fang's brutal agents.

KILDARE, CARSON and Hazard were struggling like mad to free themselves. It was all the more maddening because of Wu Fang's smile of assurance. He was positive that they couldn't escape. Hazard was hurling threats at the yellow devil. He was conscious of only one thing: they had seized Wong Chu and were going to pull him apart, torture him in the most horrible manner imaginable.

Wu Fang only smiled and directed his agents in their fiendish work. Now they had the lower ropes on the wrists of Wong Chu. The other attendant grasped his feet and began fastening the ropes from the upper bar around his ankles.

They stripped him to the waist and drew his body taut, until he ceased to struggle.

Wu Fang's fiendish smile broadened and he clasped his long-nailed hands in front of his yellow robe as he ordered, "A little tighter, please."

Wong Chu's lips were moving rapidly as he uttered a frantic prayer in Chinese. The winches tightened and his prayer ended in a scream of pain.

Wu Fang's head nodded slowly, happily. His eyes shot to the yellow executioner who held the spiked rake that was to open up the victim's body.

"Now the evil demons must leave him," Wu Fang instructed. "But—*slowly*."

The rake in the yellow beast's hand extended toward the pitiful, naked body of Wong Chu and descended. Hazard saw the jagged spikes prick the flesh cruelly. Blood spurted from the wounds, as with a horrible, leisurely movement, the yellow servant drew the spiked rake down the front of Wong Chu from his chest to his abdomen, leaving a trail of ghastly cuts in its wake.

"Again," Wu Fang ordered calmly.

At his command, the rake was raised once more. It pricked the flesh in the center of Wong Chu's body under his throat.

"That is good," Wu Fang nodded. "Our friend, Wong Chu, must not bleed to death until he has experienced all of the festive ceremony that awaits him."

Again the rake ripped the screaming, writhing Wong Chu as Wu Fang nodded to the executioners at the bar-handles.

"Now you will tighten the winches slowly," he said, "and the body will be pulled apart. But, *slowly*, remember. It is best that we proceed leisurely."

And again, Wu Fang nodded to the yellow devil with the spiked rake.

"There are more devils yet in him," he said. "Draw the rake down again."

The rake went up to the other shoulder and stabbed the flesh.

"Deeper this time," Wu Fang cooed.

The barbs dragged deeper as the arms of the Chinese assistant pressed on the rake handle. A third time the torturing implement gouged Wong Chu's body.

The agonized Chinaman opened his mouth to scream his pain and terror, but no sound would come. He had screamed until his vocal chords had given out.

The men on the winches were turning slowly, deliberately, constantly. As Hazard stared with bulging eyes, he saw Wong

Chu's body actually stretch. He was growing taller, but the arm and leg joints weren't natural; there was only flesh and skin holding them together now.

Wong Chu made no effort to scream now. His eyes glazed and his mouth sagged as total unconsciousness flooded over him. But Wu Fang permitted his men on the winches to tighten them almost another full turn, until Wong Chu was so contorted and stretched out that his form was scarcely recognizable as a human body at all. Then he stepped before the torture rack and bowed low.

When he straightened, he said, "Release him and take him away. Make ready for the next one."

Like a flash, the yellow Emperor of Death spun around and faced Jerry Hazard. His long-nailed, claw-like hands extended as he pointed straight at the newspaper man.

"I grant you the honor, Mr. Hazard," he sneered, "of being next."

CHAPTER 16
THE RECKONING

HAZARD'S BRAIN was whirling like mad. He was trying to force himself to think calmly, but he could remember no time in his life when he had been up against as ghastly a proposition as this. He could picture himself vividly, now, on the rack, being pulled apart and gouged with the spiked rake. He fought to control himself. If this was the end, he wanted to go out like a man. Wong Chu had been in mortal fear from the time he had been taken into the torture chamber. Hazard hadn't experienced quite that sensation. He had been insane with rage and hatred, but fear had not possessed him.

And now he tried to calm himself in the face of what was to come. He told himself that it would be over soon—the torture didn't last more than five or ten minutes at the most. Even ten minutes is not such a long time when you know that the torment will be over soon and Death will claim its prize.

Then he thought of Mohra and his mind leaped to the opposite angle. Again there was no definite fear, only intense hatred of Wu Fang.

Wu Fang motioned to Hazard. The newspaper man realized they were untying him. Each was a powerful fellow. They clutched his arms tightly and led him toward the rack. Hazard walked steadily, taking his punishment like a man. "You are very brave, Mr. Hazard," Wu Fang commented. "I admire you. I must admit that, no matter how much I hate you. But do not think of Mohra, for my agents will recapture her very soon and she will be all mine, when you are dead."

Those last words of Wu Fang gave sudden heart to Hazard. It meant that Mohra was still safe. Wu Fang's agents hadn't taken her yet. But they would get her if he, Kildare, and Carson died on the rack. There was no one who could take up her cause and continue to fight Wu Fang. Hazard groaned. If only he could know that Mohra would be safe!

They were now roping his hands to the knobs below with lightning speed. He felt the ropes around his ankles, then he was being drawn taut.

"A little tighter," Wu Fang was saying.

Only a few minutes, Hazard thought desperately—a few minutes of torture. He gritted his teeth as he felt the sockets of his arms and legs pulling apart. Maybe it wouldn't be so bad. He tried to make himself believe that. Perhaps it had been fright, more than anything else, that had made Wong Chu cry out the way he had.

No, this was going to be horrible! The big devil who had used the spiked rake was walking toward him. This time the yellow beast didn't have the rake. Instead, he was unsheathing a long, wickedly gleaming knife from his belt. He turned to Wu Fang.

"Master, you let me use knife?" he asked. "Very sharp. I carve him good, one slice at a time."

Wu Fang's eyes blazed and he shook his head.

"No," he said, "that would be too quick. I would not trust you with a knife."

The yellow man re-sheathed his knife obediently and picked up the rake. Wu Frank was smiling that awful, deadly smile.

"A little tighter," he said.

The winches turned, and Hazard had to clench his teeth to keep back the cry of pain that rushed to his lips.

"Now the demons must come out of his body," Wu Fang said softly.

THE RAKE descended on Hazard's body slowly—slowly. Why didn't they hurry up and get it over with? Hazard could feel cold sweat pouring out all over his body. The pain was intense as the rake came down on his flesh, gouging him with those wicked barbs.

He clenched his teeth still tighter. That wasn't so bad. He could stand that pain. If he could only thing of something else to take his mind off the torture.

Ooooh!

He couldn't keep back that groan, and it escaped even through his tightly sealed lips. The rake was going down his right side, tearing the flesh from his ribs—down over his abdomen. It burned like a million piercing needles.

They were stretching him still tighter. He mumbled a prayer between his stiff lips. He could see Wu Fang nodding to the man with the rake.

"Now another down the middle," he ordered.

The rake descended slowly. Why didn't they do it faster? Why this slow, excruciating torture? Hazard was suddenly praying that the end would come quickly. Why must he live in this awful torture?

He couldn't keep back a scream any longer, for that fiendish rake was digging deep into the flesh beneath his throat. He let out a frantic yell of desperation and agony.

Then things were happening rapidly about him! The room swam before his pain-dimmed eyes and he couldn't realize clearly what was happening. He thought he saw Mohra's face there! Yes, he was sure of it!

Dimly, he heard shots and recognized the blue-uniformed men who suddenly burst into the room as the guards who had been assigned to watch Mohra.

Then he heard Kildare yell, "Get him! Get him before he gets Mohra!"

The room was filled with struggling, fighting bodies.

Mohra screamed and more shots rang out. The room was filled with struggling, fighting bodies. There was a continuous roar of crashing forms and angry shouts, then all went black before Hazard's muddled vision.

When consciousness returned to Jerry Hazard, he was immediately aware of several things. A doctor was just turning away from him when he opened his eyes. Also in the room, which he decided immediately must be in a hospital, were Carson and Kildare. Mohra was bending over him, her lovely, dark eyes upon his.

The doctor was saying, "I can't say whether he will ever be wholly normal again. He has received a terrific shock, and that stretching ordeal that he went through has come very close to ruining him for life. He won't recover fully for months, perhaps never."

A look of awful fright flashed over Mohra's face.

"Doctor!" she gasped. "He won't die? Please say he won't!"

Her eyes filled with tears and her voice choked as she asked the question.

"No," said the doctor, shaking his head, "I'm quite sure that he won't."

Mohra whirled and dropped down on her knees beside Jerry Hazard's bed.

"What happened?" he asked.

"It all seems like a dream, now," she said. "A horrible dream. I came as soon as I found that you were in trouble. Tanya brought me word that you were going to be trapped, so I came with the police who were guarding me. You can thank Tanya for saving you."

Mohra looked up and shot a glance at Carson as she made the last remark.

"And Wu Fang?" Hazard asked. "What happened to him? Is he dead?"

Mohra nodded, but behind her, Jerry saw Val Kildare's face, and he knew that the government man wasn't so sure.

"The room caved in," Mohra told him. "It was crumbling just as I entered with the police. Mr. Kildare and Mr. Carson must have used enormous strength to pull those supports from under the top of the room. As I came in, Wu Fang made a lunge for me, but I succeeded in getting away from him. I pushed him under a wall just before it caved in."

Kildare nodded in agreement.

"They're working to get him and some of the others out now," he said. "How we ever escaped, I'll never be quite sure."

Jerry Hazard looked over at Carson. "I guess you'll have to carry on with Kildare in my place, Rod."

Carson nodded. "Yes," he said simply. He joined Kildare at the window and they both stood there, staring out into the night.

"You mustn't talk any more, Jerry," Mohra said softly. "I'm going to nurse you back to health until you are yourself again. It may take months, or years, but we'll be together always."

Hazard smiled weakly, for he felt greater joy and peace than he had ever known. The lovely dark-eyed girl bent down and gently pressed her lips to his.

Jerry Hazard slept.

POPULAR PUBLICATIONS
HERO PULPS

LOOK FOR MORE SOON!

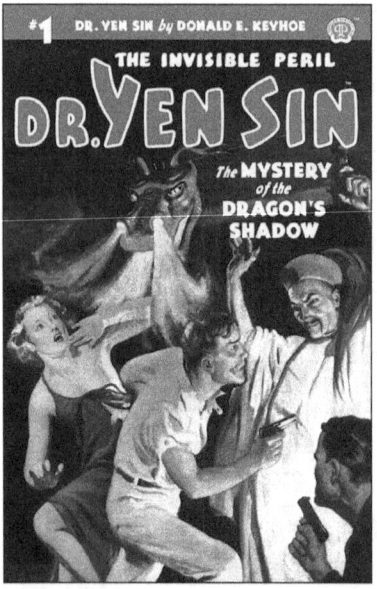

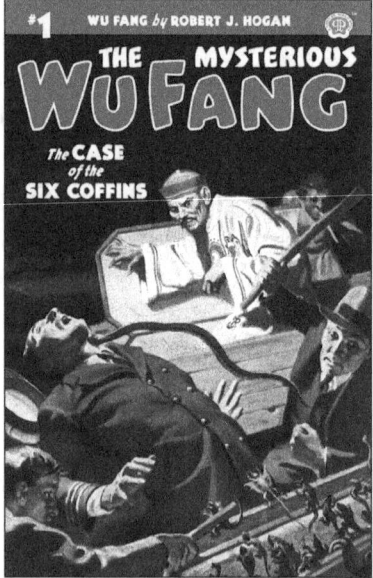